Holding On to Your Dreams

Reaching Your True Potential
In the Will of God

Bishop John C. Parks

Holding on to Your Dreams

Library of Congress

Cataloging- in- Publishing Data

ISBN:

(Paperback: 979-8-89397-540-6)

(Hardcover: 979-8-89397-541-3)

Library of Congress Card Catalog Number

1-14926480631

Published by

Bookwave Publishing

PREFACE

Dreams are the seeds from which our futures grow. They are more than fleeting thoughts or far-off fantasies—they are the whispers of divine possibility that call us to reach beyond our current limitations and dare to believe that there is more. Dreams challenge us to look past what we see and trust in what could be. They awaken purpose, stir faith, and ignite a passion to pursue something greater than you ignite. However, as beautiful as dreams are, the journey to realizing them is rarely easy. Life, with all its unpredictability, often tests the very foundation of our belief. Disappointments, delays, and detours can make us question if we ever heard God correctly or if the dream was ever real to begin with.

This book, *Holding On to Your Dreams*, is born out of a deep desire to inspire, equip, and empower you to press forward—especially when you feel like giving up. I wrote this book for those moments when your vision feels blurry, when the obstacles feel overwhelming, and when your strength feels like it is running out. Through the pages of this book, you will find encouragement to persevere through adversity, wisdom to overcome fear and self-doubt, and spiritual tools to stay rooted in faith when everything around you is shifting. You will meet people like Shanice, whose journey mirrors the complexity of holding on to a God-given dream in a world full of distractions and difficulties. Her story, and those of her friends, do not reflect a perfect picture of how to dream, but living examples of what it looks like to trust God through the process.

Ultimately, *Holding On to Your Dreams* is more than a book—it is a companion for your journey. A reminder that your dream matters, and that God—the Giver of dreams—is also the One who carries you through the waiting, the weeping, and the wondering. It's a call to align your heart with His Word and use Scripture as your roadmap, because within its pages are countless others who dared to believe, wrestled with doubt, endured hardship, and still saw the promises of God fulfilled.

If you've ever felt like letting go, if you've ever wondered if your dream is still alive, or if you simply need the strength to keep going—this book is for you. You are not alone. You are part of a great cloud of witnesses who believed against all odds. So take a deep breath. Turn the page. In addition, keep holding on.

Your dream is not over. It is only just beginning.

Bishop John C. Parks

Acknowledgement

First, I give all glory and honor to God—the ultimate Dream Giver—whose presence, promises, and providence have carried me through every chapter of this journey. Without His grace, *Holding On to Your Dreams* would not exist.

To my family, congregation of the City of Hope, and friends—thank you for being my anchor and my wings. Your unwavering love, encouragement, and belief in me have given me the courage to pursue and hold on to my dreams even when the road was hard. To my late parents, Tommie and Lela Parks, who encouraged me never to let go of my dreams.

To the dreamers, visionaries, and silent warriors who inspired these pages—this book is for you. May these words remind you that your dreams are not just possible, but necessary.

To every reader who picks up this book—I am humbled and honored to share this message with you. May it ignite hope in your heart, strengthen your faith, and push you to hold on just a little longer.

Lastly, to my editors and Sabrina Conner of Bookwave publishing who helped bring this book to life. Thank you for believing in the vision and helping me shape it into something that can bless others.

With gratitude and hope,

Bishop John C. Parks

Table of Contents

ONE

You Could be the One

"And he dreamed yet another dream and told it to his brethren, and said, I have dreamed a dream more; and behold, the sun and the moon and the eleven stars made obeisance to me." [Genesis 37:9].

Everyone has had a dream at some point in his or her life. Whether you are young or old, rich or poor, everyone has had or will have at least one intense desire to achieve or accomplish a seemingly unreachable goal. The unreachable goal occupies our minds and thoughts. We feel that supernatural ability is required to achieve these goals. These seemingly unreachable goals or strong desires become dreams.

The late afternoon sun streamed through the living room window, casting long shadows across the hardwood floor. The quiet hum of the ceiling fan did little to settle the restlessness in Shanice's spirit. She sat curled into the corner of Claudette's couch, clutching a throw pillow as if it could anchor her to something steady.

Claudette stood in the kitchen, pouring them both tea—peppermint, because that is what Shanice always asked for when she was overwhelmed. She returned and placed the steaming mug in front of her friend, then sat down opposite

1

her with a sigh that carried the weight of her own silent battles.

"Girl, you've been quiet for almost an hour," Claudette said gently. "Talk to me." Shanice stared at the cup, her hands trembling slightly as she picked it up. "I'm just... tired, Claudette. "Claudette gave her a knowing look. "Tired of what? "Shanice exhaled slowly. "Tired of hoping. Tired of pushing. Tired of acting like I know what I'm doing when really, I'm not even sure I'm on the right path."

Claudette leaned forward. "Is this about the dream?" Shanice nodded eyes suddenly glassy. "I really believed God gave it to me. However, it feels so far away now— like it is slipping through my fingers. Moreover, maybe I am able to handle it. Maybe, I need something... more. Like supernatural strength or something."

Claudette chuckled softly. "Sis, that's the whole point. You *do* need something supernatural. If you could do it in your own strength, it wouldn't be God's dream—it'd just be a project." Shanice looked up at her, eyes pleading. "But what do I do when it feels like God is silent? I went to Him last night and got nothing. I came here hoping maybe you had some kind of answer."

Claudette reached out and took her hand. "Shanice, I'm in the same storm—different boat, maybe, but still fighting the waves. I have asked God the same things. 'Why is this so hard? Why does it feel like I'm walking blindfolded?' Then He reminded me—it is not about *feeling* ready. It's about *faithfully* moving forward, even when we can't see

2

the next step." Shanice wiped her cheek with the back of her hand. "So, what do I do now?"

Claudette gave her a warm smile. "You keep pressing. Not because it is easy. Not because you feel strong. However, because deep down, you *know* God is doing something— even in the silence. Even in the delay." Shanice nodded slowly, absorbing the words. Her heart still felt heavy, but there was a flicker of peace settling in.

"I left your house earlier feeling empty," she whispered. "But now… maybe I just needed to be reminded that I'm not alone. That even when I don't feel Him, God's still up to something." Claudette squeezed her hand. "Exactly. Now, drink your tea and get ready—because we are going to take these faithful steps together. "And in that quiet room, among shared doubts and flickers of courage, the dream felt possible again.

Shanice appreciated her chance to talk to Christians of different races, backgrounds, nationalities, and countries. Most of them have or have had dreams. However, most struggle with holding on to those strong desires, aspirations, or dreams. Over time, their dreams seem to evaporate into thoughts about how things could have been. She remembers her word of the day where Apostle Paul gave her some deep insights.

The Apostle Paul's advice of pressing toward the mark of the high calling in Christ Jesus makes sense to many. However, the race seems too strenuous, and the finish line or mark seems too far away. They throw up their hands, blame the devil, and say, "What's the use?" Their dreams become dreams and thoughts that never come to fruition.

3

Shanice observed other Christians attempt to keep their faith but are unsuccessful in persevering or holding on to their dreams. Their faith seems to fizzle with time. They never realize that holding on to their dreams is an excellent demonstration of faith. For dreams, achievement is what faith is all about. Apostle Paul says in **Hebrews 11:1**.

"Faith is the substance of things hoped for (dreams), the evidence of things not seen."

Many Christians experience miracles of faith and prayer each day. They receive more blessings than they could have ever imagined. Nevertheless, they never achieve their dreams. Is this due to a lack of sincere faith? I have discovered that it is instead a lack of understanding.

Shanice took a slow sip of her tea, the warmth sliding down her throat, settling in her chest like the beginning of peace. Still, the ache had not fully left her. Her eyes drifted toward the window, where the golden light was fading into evening.

"Claudette…" she started, hesitating, "What if I've already missed it? What if I waited too long, doubted too much? What if I stepped off the path and now I don't even know how to find it again?"

Claudette did not answer right away. She sat back, letting the silence sit for a moment before speaking. "Shanice, God's not fragile. He does not abandon you because you hesitated or got confused. His purpose does not expire because of delay. But sometimes," she added, her voice soft but steady, "you need to get into the place where He

4

speaks clearly. Where you can hear Him without all the noise."

Shanice looked at her, confused. "What do you mean?"

"I mean church," Claudette said plainly. "Not for religion's sake. Not just to check a box. However, because sometimes the answers you need are waiting in His presence. Moreover, church—it is more than just a building. It's a place where your spirit can be still long enough to hear God again."

Shanice frowned slightly. "But I've prayed at home. I have read scriptures. I've listened to sermons online." "I know you have," Claudette said gently. "But there's something about *being there*. About gathering with other believers. About worship that washes over you. About hearing, a word meant for your heart in *that* moment. God speaks in different ways, Shanice. Sometimes, He sends you to the altar. Sometimes, He hides the confirmation you need in a message from someone you weren't expecting to hear it from."

Shanice set her cup down, her fingers now nervously fidgeting with the edge of her sleeve. "What if I go and still don't hear anything?" "Then you keep showing up," Claudette said firmly. "Faithful steps, remember? It is not about how you feel every time. It's about showing God you still believe He'll speak—so you position yourself to hear."

Shanice was quiet, mulling it over. Claudette reached over and tucked a strand of hair behind her ear as if a big sister would. "Go to church this Sunday," she said softly. "Don't go looking for lightning bolts. Just go expecting to hear *something*. A whisper. A word. A nudge. God honors expectation. Moreover, maybe the clarity you are waiting on is not coming at home, alone, in your confusion. Maybe, it's waiting for you in the house of God."

Shanice nodded slowly, something shifting in her. "Alright," she said finally. "I'll go." Claudette smiled, her eyes lighting up. "And I'll go with you. We're not built to walk this journey alone." Moreover, with that, a small but significant step taken. Not a leap, not a sprint—but a faithful step forward, toward the dream, and back into the presence of the One who gave it.

Therefore, Shanice went to church that Sunday to praise God for this unanticipated insight. While there, she also prayed and meditated about where God would take me next. What did God have in store for me? As the worship service began, I sat patiently, waiting for God to speak to my heart. I anxiously awaited the sermon by Pastor James H. Galloway.

Willing vessels were people that God used for His glory.

God would always show willing vessels their destiny.

Throughout her childhood, Pastor Galloway was always an inspiration. Each Sunday, he would seem to look for her after church. He reminded her to be a willing vessel for God whenever he talked to her. Pastor Galloway was emphatic that willing vessels were people God would use for His glory. God would always show willing vessels their destiny. When we are willing vessels, we open our minds to the will of God.

6

We trust God completely and firmly and believe He will keep His promises. We normally dismiss doubt and wavering faith as attacks from the enemy. As willing vessels, our minds focus so on God that we see only our preordained destiny.

That particular Sunday, Pastor Galloway preached from **Genesis 37:9**. This was the story of Jacob's youngest son, Joseph. He had occasionally preached about Joseph over the years. He had preached about Joseph's struggles and his continual favor with God. God continually elevated him. However, that Sunday, God used the story of Joseph to speak into Shanice's spirit a seed thought that would eventually change her life. In this scripture text, God revealed to Joseph his destiny through dreams.

"And he dreamed yet another dream, and told it his brethren, and said, I have dreamed a dream more; and behold, the sun and the moon and the eleven stars made obeisance to me." **[Genesis 37:9].**

Pastor Galloway pointed out that God gives us instructions through our dream thoughts. Our dream thoughts were more than wishful thinking. Our dreams are thoughts inspired by our Divine Creator. Dreams were God's way of directing our steps toward our future. **Job 33:15-17** states,

"In a dream, in a vision of the night, when deep sleep falleth upon men, in slumbering upon the bed; He openeth the ears of men, and sealeth their instructions, that He may withdraw men from his purpose, and hide pride from man."

If we remain a willing vessel, God will give us proper instructions. Many people miss these instructions because they do not understand the purpose of dreams.

At the end of the worship service, Pastor Galloway followed his custom of finding Shanice before he left the church. He encouraged her to be a willing vessel and never let go of my dreams. Pastor Galloway reiterated a key point from his sermon. In the forty-first chapter of Genesis, he affirmed that God would always provide evidence that divine favor came from Him. God would make dreams come true.

As Shanice drove home from the little wooden church that Sunday, she prayed fervently to become a willing vessel. She still had questions about her dreams. She had set goals for her life. Even though she had desires and persistent thoughts of her plans, she had never thought of these as dreams God inspired. Had God revealed her destiny to her through her dreams? As she continued to drive, she thought my goals of becoming a business executive in a major company were congruent with God's plan for my life. She became somewhat perplexed about dreams. Pastor Galloway's encouragement to become a willing vessel never departed from her heart. God would reveal their destiny to willing vessels.

The phone rang twice before Claudette answered her voice still scratchy with sleep. "Hello? "It's me," Shanice said, her voice buzzing with energy. "I couldn't wait any longer—I had to call you. "Claudette sat up. She already sensing something was different. "You okay?" "I'm better than okay," Shanice said. "Church yesterday… Claudette, it was like God had been holding that word just for me."

Claudette smiled, fully awake now. "Tell me everything."

Shanice took a breath, trying to gather her thoughts. "Pastor Galloway preached about being a *willing vessel*. Not perfect. Not powerful. Not even fully prepared. Just *willing*. Moreover, it hit me so hard—I have been waiting for some supernatural moment to make me feel ready to chase this dream. However, God is not asking for perfect conditions. He's asking for my yes." Claudette laughed softly. "Girl, that's what I've been trying to tell you."

"I know," Shanice said, her voice cracking a little. "But I needed to hear it from the pulpit. I needed to be in the atmosphere. Pastor said something like, 'God fills what's open. He uses what is available. He breathes on what's surrendered.' And it felt like every doubt I'd been holding onto got exposed." Claudette's voice softened. "So, what does this mean for you now?"

"It means I'm done hesitating," Shanice said, pacing her living room as she spoke. "I'm done waiting for signs or stars to align. I am going to be a vessel. I will show up, serve, write, speak—whatever He tells me to do; I will say yes. "Claudette smiled on the phone. "That is the Shanice, I know. Not perfect, but powerful because she's willing."

Shanice paused. "It also means I have to let go of some things. Fear. Control. The need to have all the answers. I am realizing that being a vessel means trusting the Potter. Trusting that He knows what He's pouring into me, and where He wants to pour me out." Claudette nodded, even though Shanice could not see her. "Yes. That's it right there."

9

Shanice let out a breath that sounded like freedom. "I feel lighter, Claudette. Like I finally understand what He's been trying to say all along." Claudette chuckled. "You sound lighter. Moreover, you sound ready. "I am," Shanice said confidently. "It starts now. No more waiting. I'm available."

"Well then," Claudette said with a grin in her voice, "let's go be vessels. The world doesn't know what's about to hit it." Both women laughed, and for the first time in a long time, Shanice felt like she was not chasing a dream anymore—she was walking in purpose, one faithful step at a time.

Many Christians give up on their dreams. They give up because they think their dreams are their personal goals. They have not realized that God has predestined them to become overcomers and abundantly blessed. We are also hers of an inheritance. Some things are in our destiny to fulfill. God created that "one thing" to lead us to abundant living. God has placed in each of us a gift that we can use to achieve our dreams and, ultimately, His glory. We must learn to use that: one thing." Many Christians fail because they attempt to focus on their weaknesses. While this is required, we must learn how to focus on our strengths. Joseph's gift was administrative ability. God placed Joseph in experiences to build on his strengths. Therefore, you should ask God to reveal and build upon your strengths. You will recognize your strengths. You will have a strong desire and a passion that drives you.

Our choices, faith, and determination will determine the outcome of life's situation. Our ability to keep going and patience will help us achieve the desires God has given us.

We will have to face many challenges before we reach our dreams. Yet, we will understand that all these things are necessary to develop a fuller understanding of God. These challenges will better prepare us to be good stewards of the blessings of our dreams.

So one day, Shanice thought, what is a dream? She picked up Merriam-Webster's dictionary to find a more precise definition. The dictionary defines a dream as a vision of something possible, a goal, or a purpose ardently desired to consider a possibility.

Faith in God's guarantee that our goal or purpose will become a reality by devoting our ability, zealously letting God work through us, and passionately holding on to our dreams.

The word ardently means passionate, zealous, and devoted. Then, she realized that Paul's definition of faith was broader than she knew, or experienced in her life. Dream achievement is the evidence of my faith. Things I hoped for are my dreams, goals, desires, or possibilities. **Hebrew 11:1** helped her clarify her view and understanding of dreams. In other words, faith guarantees that our supernatural goals or dreams will become a reality by

Devoting our ability, zealously allowing God to work through us, and passionately holding on until the dream happens. She felt a jolt of fire come up within her. She realized that her career and religious goals were divinely inspired. Dreams. These continual childhood thoughts were merely reflections of her destiny preordained by God.

She better understood faith and realized what God expected from her. She had to become passionate, zealous, and devoted to my dreams {Things hoped for). This is true faith. God would use her decisions or thoughts to move her toward her inheritance. Her dreams were part of her inheritance. **Ephesians 1:11** states,

"In who we have ordained an inheritance, being predestined according to the purpose of him who worketh all things after the counsel of his will."

God predestined our future. Bad choices and decisions and resulting circumstances only hinder us but do not prevent us from achieving our divine purpose. All great patriarchs and saints had a predestined future.

At first glance, the patriarchs' destinies were a collection of missteps and bad decisions. However, the mighty hand of God was always working. Their challenge was to allow God to direct their every step. Solomon gives us good advice in the book of Proverbs. Solomon stated that everything is vanity. However, we can only trust God. **Proverbs 3:6** emphasizes this point,

"Trust in the Lord with all thine heart; and lean not to thine understanding. In all thine ways acknowledge Him, and He shall direct your path."

God is committed to direct our path. However, God wants you to trust Him completely. God expects you to show appreciation and gratitude {Acknowledgment) for His grace given to you.

The first step toward achieving your dreams is realizing that you are pre-destined for greatness. This is one point that many Christians miss. They know that Jesus came and that we might have life and life more abundantly. Yet, they fail to see that the more abundant they are, the more they represent achieving supernatural things. Your dreams should be more significant than a loving family, a good job, a car, a house, clothes, and friends. Many Christians believe that these things represent the pinnacle of success. We must realize that this dream falls far from what God wants us to achieve. Our personal goals will fall short of the inheritance God has preordained for us.

As God revealed this about dreams to her, she began studying Joseph's steps to hold onto his dreams. God placed this story in the Bible to show us his blueprint for achieving our destiny. Let us examine God's blueprint for Joseph.

At an early age, Joseph dreamed of his future. In **Genesis 37:9,** Joseph saw himself as God saw him. Joseph would become the head and not the tail. He would become above only and not beneath. Joseph said, "I have dreamed a dream more; and, behold, the sun and the moon and the eleven stars made obeisance to me." Joseph's thoughts were more than wishing thinking. Joseph realized that these were instructions from God. His family disregarded his comments, but God was affirming Joseph's destiny. Joseph saw himself, as he would become. How do you see yourself? You cannot just see yourself just as blessed. You must see yourself actually blessed exceedingly, abundantly; above all, you can ask or think. Is this what dreams are really about? They are not normal thoughts about achieving everyday things. Dreams are thoughts

13

about the achievement of marvelous and supernatural things. Your dreams should exceed mere overachieving. If God inspires your dreams, they it should be about achieving the impossible things.

You must begin seeing yourself as God sees you. See yourself blessed exceedingly, abundantly, above all you can ask or think. In a quiet moment of reflection, Shanice begins to think about the nature of her dreams. She realizes that she cannot afford to see herself through a limited lens anymore. She cannot just believe in succeeding—she must see herself *blessed exceedingly, abundantly above all she could ask or think.* This revelation becomes her new insight: those true, God-given dreams are not ordinary or safe—they are bold, supernatural, and meant to exceed the boundaries of logic and possibility.

Her inspiration is now rooted in divine expectation. Shanice understands that if God inspires her dreams, they must reach beyond comfort and routine. They must be visions of the impossible made possible—mountains moved, doors opened, and impact made in ways that only Heaven could orchestrate.

With this clarity, Shanice feels a fire rise within her. She is no longer chasing goals for the sake of success—she is chasing the kind of vision that transforms lives and glorifies God. In addition, that changes everything.

Your dreams may seem unattainable at first glance. They may appear as wishful thinking and possibilities. However, you must begin to see yourself entirely as God

14

sees you. God sees beyond where you are. He knows your true potential. He allows tests to occur as part of your development. Each test intends to make you stronger, more confident, and closer to Him. If you do not resist and remain obedient to His will, you will achieve your success and destiny. The Bible has scriptures on how God sees you. You must see yourself in God's way for the achievement of your dreams. Only when you see yourself in God's way will God begin to move you toward your inheritance.

Stop and meditate on this thought for a minute. You could be the one. You could be the one God is waiting to unleash for His glory. There are so many powerful and anointed men and women of God. These notable Christians include Bishop TD Jakes, Billy Graham, Kenneth Copeland, Creflo Dollar, and Joyce Myers, to name a few. Have you ever listened closely to each of their testimonies? They all had dreams,

You could be the one that God is waiting to unleash.

More than that. They each see themselves as God sees them. You should not discount your true potential. Your outcome will depend on how you feel about yourself. So, why not you? God wants to do more than you can think or ask. It is according to the working of the power that is in you. You must expand your faith to believe you. It could be the one. Otherwise, God's instructions will not make sense to you.

After Joseph's revelation, he began behaving as if his dreams were already a reality, not a possibility. Joseph spoke with so much confidence that his brothers became envious of him. Joseph was so convinced that even Jacob, his father, became upset. Yet, Joseph's confidence made Jacob notice his son and keep the matter in mind.

Most Christians have read or heard about positive thinking. However, God wants you to think with the power of His anointing. You must become familiar with the concept of "victory thinking." This kind of thinking is more powerful. Positive thinking attempts to motivate you to think optimistically about your possibilities. However, victory thinking causes you to start your journey with the end in mind. You behave as if the outcome of your dream is a reality now. Victory thinking will prevent you from focusing on the present surroundings. You can only see the achievement of supernatural success.

Victory thinking is thinking and speaking with confidence of the outcome as though it is reality now.

Only through victory thinking could the three Hebrew boys stand fearless while facing a fiery furnace. Victory thinking also enabled Paul and Silas to conduct a midnight revival while held captive in a Philippian jail. John the Revelator remained faithful while exiled on the island of Patmos. Other great saints were born into poverty and oppression. Victory thinking helped them overcome the odds.

Despite his obstacles and afflictions, Joseph never stopped thinking of victory. Nowhere in the Scriptures do you see Joseph mired by his circumstances. Each circumstance reinforced his resolve. Joseph received the favor of God because of his willingness to think victoriously. He knew he could overcome by putting his total trust in the Almighty God. So, how do you initiate victory thinking? It is simple. It starts with your mind. It begins with faith. Remember Shanice's revelation on the definition of faith. Faith guarantees that our supernatural goal or dream will become a reality by devoting our ability, zealously letting God work through us, and passionately holding on until the dream happens. When we begin to think of our dreams victoriously, we devote our ability to the achievement of our dreams while zealously allowing God to work through us. Then, God will reaffirm our thoughts through revelations by the Holy Spirit.

Though victory thinking, you must think with confidence of a supernatural outcome. Your victory thinking reaffirmed the revelations given to you by the Holy Spirit. **I Corinthians 2:9-10** states;

"Eye has neither seen nor ear heard nor have entered into the heart of man, the things which God hath prepared for them that love him. But God hath revealed them unto us by His Spirit; for the Spirit searcheth all things, yea, and the deep things of God."

Once God shows you your destiny through the Holy Spirit, you must begin thinking, speaking, and preparing for your dreams. The power of victory thinking will make your dream move toward you. The more you passionately believe, speak, and act on them, and the more zealous you are about achieving them, the faster they will happen.

Without a doubt, you could be the one. God has already declared that He is no respecter of persons. God perfects his will through your thoughts and your spoken word. The Bible even tells us that God's angels await us to speak a word that will call them into action. You must think and speak of your dream in the present tense and not the future tense. Joseph was so convinced that he began telling his dream publicly. Joseph's thinking and speaking about his dreams reaffirmed his confidence in the God of promise. When you embrace victory thinking, you are demonstrating true faith in God. Victory thinking motivates God to keep His covenants.

What did Joseph think and say? Joseph only thought and talked about the outcome of his dreams. This is a wonderful thing. God will not reveal the steps for His master plan for your life. These steps are in God's mind. Joseph would never have volunteered for his tribulation. However, his tribulation created his opportunity. His opportunity created his destination, and his destination took him to the achievement of his dreams.

We cannot interfere with God's plan when we are unaware of the steps to our dreams. By nature, we always try to take control of our lives. We must restrain ourselves from this type of behavior. We have to learn how to allow God to order our steps. Much of how we think depends on the teaching we receive. How did you receive experience? People teach us to be proactive and take charge of our lives. These principles are correct in achieving our plans. However, they often hinder us from achieving our dreams. Even though we may think we have thought out the plan, God still directs our every step.

Joseph did not create a twelve-step plan for achieving his dreams. Joseph left those details to the Lord. Joseph had continual thoughts of supernatural success. Then, Joseph used every opportunity God led him through to gain experience and spiritual maturity. Each experience or situation took him one-step closer to his dreams. So, one of your most significant challenges will be to resist interfering in God's plan for your life. **Psalms 37:23** states;

"The Lord orders the steps of a good man or woman, and he delights in his way."

The more passionately you speak about your dream; and the more zealous you are toward achieving it; will determine how fast it will happen.

God orders our steps. He determines the pace, hurdles, and milestones on your journey. Eventually, you learn to trust Him completely. You understand that God knows what He is doing. God knows what is ahead. He will lead you through it. God knows where the curves are. He knows the necessary trials to increase your patience and endurance. Your role is to remain—patient and enduring. You must remain passionate, zealous, and devoted to the dream. Remember, the revelations.

God gave me on faith a few pages back. The most excellent demonstration of your faith is making your dreams a reality by devoting ability, zealously letting God work through you, and passionately holding on to your dream. No matter what happens, you must hold onto your dream.

Despite all the struggles, disappointments, and trials, Joseph remained steadfast that God would work all things together for the good. You must be convinced that you will arrive at your appointed predestination. You must be determined that you could be the one. You could be the one God prepares to unleash supernatural blessings. Those thoughts, desires, or inspirations have already been born. Now, you must take the first step. You could be the one who will testify about the achievement of supernatural success. Through your testimony and success, others will see that dreams come true.

God is looking for willing vessels to give Him glory and honor, and for someone to bless Him with supernatural blessings. What would happen if God blessed you?

Shanice could not hold it in—she had to share what was stirring in her spirit. She picked up the phone and called Claudette, her trusted friend and spiritual sister, who had walked with her through both dry seasons and seasons of overflow. As soon as Claudette answered, Shanice's words came pouring out.

"Girl," she began, "I've been seeing things differently lately. It is as if something clicked. I can't just see myself as blessed—I have to see myself as *exceedingly, abundantly* blessed... like, *beyond* anything I've ever imagined. In addition, I realize now that if God inspires my dreams, they are supposed to be big. Supernatural. Wild even."

Claudette listened closely, nodding even though Shanice could not see her. "That's it right there," she said. "God-sized dreams will always stretch us. That's the real test."

Their conversation shifted into sacred ground as they began to talk about the *keys to holding on* when the vision feels distant:

1. Guard Your Mind. Claudette reminded Shanice, "You have to protect your thoughts. Doubt creeps in when your mind is open to fear, comparison, and negativity. Meditate on what God said—*not* what the situation looks like."

2. Speak Life Daily. They both agreed: your words frame your reality. Shanice shared how she started declaring Scripture over her dreams every morning, especially **Ephesians 3:20.** "Speaking life reminds me of who God is—*and* who I am in Him."

3. Surround Yourself with Vision Carriers. "That's why I called you," Shanice laughed. "I need people who see what I see... even when it's still in seed form." Claudette affirmed, "You can't share big dreams with small-minded people. You need midwives, not critics."

4. Take Faith Steps. They talked about how obedience in the small things builds momentum. Claudette said, "Sometimes, holding on means moving forward—one step at a time—even if it doesn't all make sense yet."

By the end of their conversation, they were both encouraged, empowered, and reminded that holding on is not passive—it is a posture of faith, expectation, and endurance. Before hanging up, Shanice said, "I don't know what's next, but I know I'm not letting go. These dreams aren't just mine... they're Heaven-breathed." Claudette smiled, "And if Heaven breathed them, Heaven will bring them to life."

TWO

Detours Can Lead to Destiny

"And Joseph was brought down to Egypt; and Potiphar, as an officer of Pharaoh, captain of the guard, an Egyptian, bought him off the hands of the Ishmaelite, which brought him down thither. And the Lord was with Joseph, and he was in Egypt; and Potiphar, and he was in the house of his master the Egyptian." Genesis 39:1, 2.

It is amazing how God orchestrates our steps. We often stop to wonder, "How did I get here?" Each decision led to another situation, and each situation led to another person or opportunity. Most of the time, we think we are taking a detour away from our dream.

Shanice sat across from her father, Carlos, on a quiet Saturday afternoon. They were at their favorite coffee shop, tucked into a corner booth with warm drinks in hand. The atmosphere was peaceful, but Shanice's heart was full of reflection and revelation. She had realized she could no longer keep to herself.

"Daddy," she began, stirring her tea absentmindedly, "I've been thinking a lot about my journey lately. For a while, I thought I was off track… as if I had missed it. You know— missed my moment, missed God." Carlos looked at her, his eyes soft and wise. "What made you feel that way, baby?"

Shanice sighed. "Because everything I planned didn't happen as I thought it would. I had this idea of where I was supposed to be by now. However, life took a turn. Moreover, I thought I had messed it up for a long time. However, lately… I've been seeing it differently." Carlos leaned in, listening closely.

Shanice continued her voice steady. "I thought it was a detour. Now I see—it was *direction*. What I thought was a delay was divine development. The places I ended up, the people I met, the things I learned—it was all God. He was ordering my steps even when I didn't understand them."

Carlos nodded slowly, a proud smile forming on his face. "That's the beauty of walking with God," he said. "Sometimes, He lets us think we're lost… just to show us we were right where we needed to be."

Shanice smiled, tears threatening the corners of her eyes. "It's crazy, Daddy. I thought I had taken a wrong turn. However, what I called a detour, God was calling destiny. Every disappointment, every delay, every redirection—it all served a purpose."

Carlos reached across the table and took her hand. "That's called *maturity*, sweetheart. Learning to trust the process. Detours may not be comfortable, but they are often the road that leads us to our purpose. God doesn't waste anything—not a moment, mistake, or even heartbreak."

Shanice nodded. "I needed that. I did. I'm starting to believe again… and dream again, but this time with faith that even the unexpected roads can still get me there."

Carlos grinned, "That's my girl. Remember, it's not always the straight path that leads you to destiny—it's the surrendered one."

They sat there a little longer in silence, the kind that feels full and sacred. Shanice left that conversation lighter, stronger, and more assured that she wasn't off course—she was right on time, walking the winding road that God Himself had paved with purpose.

During these last few months, Joseph's life gave Shanice a key revelation. Detours can lead to destiny. What seemed like a detour to another company was positioning her. God was strategically moving her toward her destiny. He was directing her intently so that one event could lead to another. The mighty hand of God orchestrated her entire detour.

Most try to position themselves for the best opportunities, places, and people. Usually, this approach is a wasted effort. God creates the opportunity. God had little David carry lunch to his brothers, so that God could have David fight Goliath. David's detour to the battlefield was a step toward his destiny in the King's palace. Rejoice in every detour. Each detour is an opportunity for God.

Examine the detour that Joseph took. Joseph was destined to become the Governor of Egypt. His dream spoke of the sun, moon, and stars bowing down to him **[Genesis 37:9]**. However, God did not catapult him into his destiny. He took a 13-year detour. Joseph's detours took him into a variety of difficult situations. Without knowing how the story would turn out, one would think Joseph's dreams were completely off track.

By nature, we try to avoid trials, tribulations, and temporal afflictions. These things do not feel good. However, detours are part of God's master plan and serve a greater purpose [James 1:2-4].

The testing of your faith or detours helps you develop perseverance. Perseverance makes you mature and completely lacking nothing. Your detours help your spiritual growth, as you gain the necessary experience and maturity.

Joseph had two major detours that led to his destiny. Joseph moved from being his father's pet to a pit. Then, Joseph moved from being a slave to a servant. Jacob's favorite son was Joseph. He was one of the two sons born by Rachel,

Our desires Help our Spiritual growth So that We can gain the necessary experience.

whom Jacob loved until her death. Jacob gave Joseph a coat of many colors as a testimonial of his father's love. Yet, these blessings led him to end up in a pit. However, please note that Joseph could have only arrived in Egypt in Pharaoh's house because his brethren put him in a pit. Your pit is God's way of isolating you to get you on track. When you find yourself seemingly stuck in a seemingly

hopeless situation, you should be rest assured that God is up to something. God is attempting to redirect you in some way. This is how God positions you for the next step in your journey to your dreams.

You must learn to accept where God has temporarily placed you. Your pet is only temporary. You must learn to be content until God gets ready to take you to your next steps. Paul tells us in **Philippians 4:11.**

"Not that I speak in respect of want, for I have learned in whatsoever state I am, therewith to be content."

You must resist the urge to rationalize and figure out your deliverance. God had to maneuver Joseph in place so that Joseph would be in the right place. Joseph would never leave Canaan on his own. Joseph was at home, living comfortably with his entire family and friends. However, Joseph's destiny was in the palace. Joseph's pit isolated him from the things and the people that could ultimately hinder him. Therefore, God arranged a journey into a pit. Interestingly, it was the people closest to him that put him there. However, the mighty hand of God was working on his behalf.

Father's Pet to Pit

This part of Joseph's life explains many things. As Christians, we feel like our heavenly Father's pet. Our heavenly Father consistently demonstrates to us that He loves us. He always treats us special. He blesses us despite our temperament or spiritual maturity. Most of our blessings are unexpected and undeserved. These blessings are God's way of giving us a coat of many colors. The coat of many colors shows our friends, family, co-workers, and community that we are unique. God anoints, appoints, and approves us. We rejoice in these things. We feel confident that God is with us. We hurriedly get to church to praise Him and say thank you in a public assembly. We think uniquely to the point that we believe that little harm would ever come to us.

As our Father's pet, we ask God for special privileges and blessings. God seems to answer our every prayer. He gives us a favor that permits us to meet our goals effortlessly. We have friends, family, and favors. What else could a child ask of their Father? When we look for an opportunity to follow our Father's will, our world changes dramatically. We find ourselves in a pit. Many times, we are there unawares. We blame the devil, people, or bad decisions. We feel isolated from our God. Our dreams seem to stop in the pit. We cannot move forward. Every Christian must realize that God will allow us to enter a pit. Our pit is not to harm us. The pit is into help us. I know that my years of struggle were my pit. A pit will be on your journey toward achieving your dreams. You should not even ask God, "why me?" The devil will show up while you are in your pit. He will make you believe God did you wrong or that you are lacking in your relationship with God. However, our pit is only temporary.

Every pit, whether financial problems, issues with relationships, or health problems, is a "pit." For His glory. God used our pit to isolate us so that we could change directions. God revealed to me other saints that He allowed them to get into the pit and become isolated so that He could move them closer to their destiny.

MOSES. Moses' pit became the backside of a desert. Moses had to leave a plush palace to live forty years as a shepherd watching over someone else's sheep. However, it was at the backside of a mountain isolated, and seemingly going nowhere, that Moses met God. When

Moses was isolated from his people, God could speak to Moses' heart. Then, God moved him to his ultimate assignment – Israel's deliverance.

JACOB. Jacob's pit was living in the desert far from home and his father's house. Jacob stole his brother's birthright and became a fugitive. He could not return home. However, it was in his isolation that he met God and received blessings, and a divine name change to Israel.

The Bible contains many resumes of people that God allowed to get in a pit, so that He could change their direction. Therefore, whenever you find yourself in a pit, you should realize that God wants to isolate you so that He can redirect your steps.

The Ishmaelites bought Joseph as a slave. When we are in a pit, we become a slave to whatever God is using to change us. The pit captures us and nothing can deliver us, until the appointed time and place. Early in life, Shanice thought these situations were of the devil. Then, the Holy Spirit revealed the difference to her. We find the revelation in the story of Joseph. When God captures you, nothing can harm you because God is using the people, place, or thing. You may feel helpless and lack control of the situation. However, you should remember that God has to capture you to carry you to the next steps. When the devil is involved, you will see destruction and calamity. Remember, that the devil comes to steal, kill, and destroy. If the devil captures us, his will is that your life spirals on a downward plight to destruction. However, when God captures you, He is preparing you for a greater purpose. You may have to endure a temporal affliction, but favor is still on your life. **Genesis 39:2** reminds us that the Lord was with Joseph.

Notice that Joseph traveled to Egypt as a slave, but immediately became a servant in his place of destiny. Shanice had to learn this interesting fact about God. God always places us in the place of our destiny to be a servant.

We must resist the urge to ask God why we have to become a servant. Why does God locate us in certain places with certain types of people? In many respects, we may have become a servant to people with less anointing, less gifts, and less favor with God. However, God has to teach us some things about servanthood. Upon arrival into Egypt, Potiphar, an officer of Pharaoh, purchased Joseph as a servant. Shanice had to know more. She picked up her Bible and turned to Genesis 39 to see what God was saying to her.

When she read **Genesis 39:2**, she received a powerful revelation from God: "and he (Joseph) was in the house of his master the Egyptians." God connected Joseph to the right house. He gained knowledge, credibility, and integrity. This is what servanthood teaches us. You cannot simply arrive at your destiny without the proper knowledge and experience. God uses servanthood to teach us responsibility, to refine our skills, and ability. Servanthood allows you to become credible with people, while your experience is growing. Without being a servant first, you will not properly be prepared to handle your position of leadership.

Look how God prepared Joseph for an ultimate position by reading **Genesis 39:4, 6.**

Joseph learned how to oversee Potiphar's household and all his possessions. Remember, God first proves to us we are trustworthy with another man's riches before He will give you the true riches of your dream. This is part of servanthood training. Joseph was now favored with all of Potiphar's household and acquaintances. As you go through your training in servanthood, you must learn all you can. Remember, God uses all things working together for your good. Servanthood intention is to humble you. You will experience your deepest emotions and levels of anxiety. Servanthood also helps others to see your growth. During this period, your skills and ability are being fine-tuned. Your experiences are exacting a perfect work in you. Without servanthood training, you would not appreciate the blessings from God. More importantly, you would not be able to help others understand the benefits of trials and tribulations. A testimony without experience is like clouds with no rain. As you move through your phases of servanthood, you should rejoice.

Joseph's experience in servanthood was beneficial to him as he faced his greatest challenges. He would not have been equipped to administrate through a calamity without this experience. Without servanthood training, you would not be capable of sustaining our dream, even if by happenchance you achieved it. You should remember to disregard the circumstances, your surroundings, or the people you have association with. Your motivation is to use servanthood training for a greater purpose.

As Shanice sat with the weight of her revelation from **Genesis 39:2**, she felt a still, small voice stir in her spirit. It was not just about recognizing God's presence in the middle of her process—it was about **staying the course**.

She leaned back in her chair, eyes lifted slightly, and whispered,

"Okay, God… I see it now. You are with me *here*, I do not need to rush to 'there.' I do not have to manipulate outcomes or panic when things feel slow. You're not just with me in the promise—you're with me in the process." Then the next thought hit her like a gentle but firm nudge: "Stay the course, Shanice." She knew exactly what it meant. Stay faithful. Stay planted. Stay hopeful. Even when it does not look like it is working. Even when nothing seems to be moving. Because God's presence is the proof that things are happening—even when we cannot see them.

She thought about Joseph again. He stayed the course through betrayal, false accusations, prison, and delay. Yet, in every chapter, the Lord was with him. Each test was preparing him for the throne—and each step was part of the strategy.

Shanice nodded to herself, almost smiling. "I won't jump ship just because I don't see the shore. If God is with me, then this season is not a waste. It's a setup."

From that moment forward, "stay the course" became her heart's instruction and her soul's anchor. She would continue showing up, trusting, believing, and walking— even through the unfamiliar—because the same God who was with Joseph in the pit and the prison was walking with her now. Moreover, that was more than enough.

THREE

Don't Let Obstacles Stop You

"And it came to pass after these things that his master's wife cast her eyes upon Joseph, and she said lie with me. In addition, it happened, as she spoke to Joseph day by day, which he hearkened not unto her, to lie with her, or to be with her. **Genesis 39:7, 10.**

Joseph was goodly and well favored in Potiphar's house. Potiphar trusted Joseph with all of his possessions. Joseph could have become complacent and thought that Potiphar's house was the achievement of his dreams. This is a trap for most Christians. They achieve the American dream and become satisfied with their blessings. These Christians stop short of their true potential in the will of God. They have a job or career, people respect them, and they become content with their achievements. Some are amazed that they were able to make it this far. When they compare themselves to other Christians, they have surpassed the average Christian.

What more could they ask for? They justify their contentment by rationalizing that God does not want us to be rich, or the love of money is the root of all evil deeds. Therefore, they stop dreaming, become content, and never reach their true potential in the will of God. These people are also the ones who harbor regret later in their life. They finally realize that God wanted more for them. Usually, they see someone that had less natural ability exceed them.

Unfortunately, they become unwilling to step out on faith, and reinvigorate their dream. They lack the motivation, confidence, and energy. Their dream evaporates.

We must understand that God is committed to us fulfilling our dreams. If we persevere and stay within the will of God, we will receive the promise. For those people like Joseph who do not want to become complacent, they will continue to strive and excel, knowing God will elevate them to achieve even greater levels of anointing through Him. God is able to do exceedingly, abundantly above all that you can ask or think. However, this type of anointing is the power that is within you. As a Christian, you must maintain your integrity. You must completely understand that accomplishing your dreams glorifies God. The Bible says in **St. Matthew 16:19:**

"So, let your light so shine that men may see your good works and glorify God in heaven."

When you excel in abundant good works or the accomplishment of your dreams, God gets the glory out of your life. Then, others begin to see what God has done for you. Your blessings help increase someone's faith in God.

If you do not stop and dwell at the crossroad of complacency, the next steps on the journey to your dreams are the trying of your faith. God will evaluate our faith in Him. Therefore, God allows obstacles to test you. So, what does God test? God reveals to us the nature of our patience and self-control **[Hebrews 10:36].**

God sees obstacles to build our patience. The obstacles test our faith. God wants to see whether we will stay within His

33

will. Many times, we fail the test. Therefore, God allows us to see the same obstacles repeatedly until we overcome them.

Many Christians give up at this point and begin to accept the status quo. Their testimonies are outdated and speak of things that happened many years ago. Many become disillusioned with God while they watch others achieve their dream. They believe that God has let them down. However, those who see themselves in their dream and realize that God is testing them will persevere. Even though God anoints, appoints, and approves us, we must pass the temptations and trials.

Verse 7 of the 39th chapter of Genesis says, "And it came to pass after these things, that." Moreover, the fact that it happened suggests some kind of prearranged situation that God was allowing to happen. God created a hedge around Joseph while he was gaining favor and control of Potiphar's house.

Obstacles will take one of three forms: lust of the flesh, pride, or fear.

The bible now indicates something happened. After these things, the blessings and favor materialized in Joseph's life. Then, it happened. God always evaluate what choices we will make. God wants to know we will maintain our integrity, and remain tenacious toward achieving our dreams. Therefore, the first test is always a test of patience.

Would Joseph remain devoted to God and Potiphar? Therefore, it happened.

34

God knew that obstacles could distract or sidetrack Joseph. If Joseph did not possess patience, he would fail. In my life experiences, I have learned that every obstacle allowed me to become distracted, preoccupied, or give up. God allows the devil to construct these obstacles for a greater purpose. The devil's ultimate desire is to stop us.

These obstacles will take three forms: lust of the flesh, pride, or fear. The devil will exploit our weaknesses by exploiting one or all of these obstacles. Throughout the Bible, these three obstacles appear, even in the temptation of Jesus in the wilderness. The fourth chapter of Matthew details the barriers that Satan used against Jesus. It is very important on your journey to your destiny that you familiarize yourself with Satan's obstacles. Satan said in Matthew, chapter 4,

"If thou be the Son of God, command that these stones be made bread." [Lust of the Flesh].

"If thou be the Son of God, cast thyself down; for it is written, He shall give His angels charge concerning thee; and in their hands they shall bear thee up, lest at any time thou dash thy foot against a stone." [Fear].

"And he saith unto him, all these things will I give thee, if thou wilt fall and worship me." [Pride].

There are more examples throughout the Bible revealing these three obstacles as Satan's primary weapons. The devil attempts to show God that his investment in and love for us are futile.

Take a minute to think about your obstacles. You should be able to categorize all of your trials, tribulations, or tests in one of these categories. Remember, the devil has no new tricks. The Apostle Paul instructs not to be ignorant of the devil's devices **[2 Corinthians 2:11]**.

Therefore, we must always be watchful and prayerful of these obstacles.

Examine verse seven of Genesis 39 in Joseph's story again, and it happened. Whenever we see these words in the Holy Scripture, it is an indication of some temporary event. The event happened. It did not come to stay. God lets you know that you can prevail over your obstacles. No temptation or test comes to stay. The obstacle is God's way of allowing you to grow in maturity. You have to maintain complete and unwavering faith in God. Your goal ought to be to increase your patience. Patience helps you endure every obstacle. Let us examine these three enemies of our soul in Joseph's journey to his dream.

Pride

Joseph could have yielded to pride. Look at his accomplishments in just a few years.

- He went from enslaved person to servant in Potiphar's house. The LORD was with Joseph and greatly blessed him in all his endeavors.
- Joseph became Potiphar's favorite. Potiphar put Joseph in charge of his entire household and entrusted him with all of his businesses.

- The LORD blessed Potiphar for Joseph's sake. Potiphar gave Joseph complete control over everything that he owned.

Joseph could have already yielded to pride. As a youth, he had a deep-seated pride. Joseph was babied, pampered, and spoiled. All of this had gone to Joseph's head. His pride led to his brothers planning to murder him. Often, pride leads us to believe that our gift or ability has created an opportunity. We thank God for the blessings, but praise ourselves for the accomplishment. It is so easy to think that our hard work made us successful.

Pride is the root and essence of sin. The fall of Adam and Eve centered on pride. Adam and Eve desired to be "like God." Pride seeks for oneself the honor and glory that properly belong to God. Pride is conceit concerning one's talents, ability, wealth, or position in life. Pride always leads to disdainful behavior and disobedience. Pride caused the devil and one-third of the heaven host of angels to rebel against God.

The devil uses pride because he knows how God feels about pride [Proverbs 8:13]. God hates pride. We must beware of the obstacle of pride. Pride puts us at odds with God. Pride is the ringleader of many other sins. For pride lies within our hearts. Therefore, God used Joseph's struggles to help him overcome pride. Joseph's struggles caused him to replace his pride with a humble spirit. Regardless of your success, always acknowledge that God is the source and sustainer of all good and perfect gifts.

Lust of the Flesh

The second obstacle is the lust of the flesh. Satan will always appeal to our flesh. He will tempt us to yield through temptations or pressures. Lust of the flesh is any intense desire that becomes excessive or misdirected. It may be concentrated on money, personal power, or sensual pleasures, such as sexual experiences and drunkenness. Again, Satan used this same obstacle in Adam and Eve. **Genesis 3:6** says;

"And the woman saw that the tree was good for food, and that it was pleasant to the eyes, and a tree to be desired to make one wise, she took of the fruit thereof, and did eat, and gave also unto her husband with her; and he did eat."

The tree was pleasant to the eye and created the temptation. The temptation turned into lust. So, lust of the flesh is a key weapon of Satan.

In Joseph's case, Potiphar's wife attempted to have sex with him. Potiphar's wife kept tempting and putting pressure on him day after day. Joseph refused to sleep with her, and he kept out of her way as much as possible. Sometimes, merely trying to say no to the temptation is not enough. We must be watchful and avoid the temptation completely, especially when the temptation is strong and persistent. Joseph resisted the temptation by acknowledging that it would be a sin against God. Joseph refused to disobey God. He would destroy his relationship with God. Joseph proved to God that he could be trusted more and more a higher position of leadership.

Under pressure, we rationalize excuses away. Remember, the devil's intention is to create disobedience to God. Disobedience to God separate us from the favor of God. This is how we allow hindrances to sidetrack us away from our dreams. Yielding to the lusts will create strongholds, and ultimately war with the soul.

"Dearly beloved, I beseech you as strangers and pilgrims abstain from fleshly lusts, which war against the soul." [I Peter 2:11].

Joseph was stronger through this persistent temptation. God allowed Joseph to be tempted, so that he could learn self-denial, and self-control. Lust of the flesh attempts to rob us of control of our body, thoughts, and sanctification.

Fear

The third obstacle to reaching our dreams is fear. Fear paralyzes us and demonstrates a lack of faith. Fear is the opposite of faith. God promotes faith, and the devil promotes fear. Many Christians stop on their journey to their dreams due to fear. They become fearful of the outcome or possible tragedy. They are unwilling to confront those things that are attempting to hinder them. Public opinion or the desire to have no pain makes them walk cautiously in every endeavor.

Joseph's real test occurred after he was successful. He would have to make decisions that either would lead him to his dreams, or become sidetracked. Becoming successful does not eliminate your fears. Success creates the opportunity for fear to exploit your faith. Joseph could have become fearful of Potiphar's wife and yielded to her seduction. Joseph was in a serious predicament. What was he to do? If he submitted and yielded to Potiphar's wife, he probably could have gained a great advantage that could result in her favor. However, if he refused her, he could know her wrath. He could ultimately lose all of his blessings awarded to him. I would imagine Joseph had to contemplate deeply his course of action. Saying no to Potiphar's wife could lead to imprisonment or death.

One day, not all of the menservants were available in the house. When Joseph entered in the house to perform his daily business, Potiphar's wife grabbed him and propositioned him. To deny her probably would have meant arousing her wrath and vengeance. However, Joseph ran out of the house. Joseph fled so quickly that she yanked his cloak off.

Sometimes, the evil seduces Christians through fear. These Christians begin to feel that they will end up losing something valuable. Therefore, the devil takes advantage of their fear. The devil attempted to use fear on Job, a perfect and upright man. In the book of Job, Job said that the thing that feared had come upon him,

"For the thing which I greatly feared is come unto me [Job 3:25]."

Fear is not from God. The Bible says that God has not given us the spirit of fear. We should never allow fear of failure to make us lose confidence in God.

Psalms 23:4 says; "Yea, though I walk through the valley of the shadow of death, I will fear no evil."

The obstacle of fear is one of Satan's greatest weapons. The devil knows that without faith, it is impossible to please God. Unfortunately, fear normally comes when we speak it into existence. You cannot talk or walk in fear. Whatever you fear will come upon you. When we walk in faith, we believe in God. When we have fear, we believe in the devil.

Fear does not come from God. Scripture instructs us that God has given us the spirit of love, power, and a sound mind. We can only overcome the obstacles of fear by completely trusting in God. Not yielding to our fears may create a new trial for us. However, the God of promise will always make a way to escape.

Joseph was able to overcome all of his obstacles. This is a crucial part of holding on to your dreams. Your willingness to face your obstacles and deal with them, will determine your ultimate outcome. If you attempt to move around your obstacles, it will result in delay. Eventually, you will face the same obstacles that you attempted to avoid. This is part of God's process of maturing us. Therefore, you should plan to face obstacles. If you wrestle with them, you will overcome them by the power of God.

Anchoring the Vision: Confronting Obstacles to Fulfill the Dream

Shanice sat alone on the edge of her bed, her phone resting in her hand like a weight. The room was quiet, except for the hum of the ceiling fan and the quiet tapping of her foot against the hardwood floor. Her mind was anything but still. For days, maybe weeks now, a single thought had been stirring inside her, growing louder with every passing moment: *You cannot move forward without facing what you have been running from.*

The realization unsettled her. She had always prided herself on being positive, resilient, always pressing forward. However, what she had not admitted until now was that her version of "pressing forward" often meant sidestepping the hard things. Avoiding conflict. Dodging discomfort. Pretending that obstacles did not exist if she did not give them her attention.

However, dreams do not grow in the dark. They grow in truth. Moreover, she knew she needed to talk to someone who understood that better than anyone she knew—her father. With a hesitant breath, Shanice unlocked her phone and dialed his number. "Hey baby girl," Carlos answered, his voice warm and steady, like always. "Hey, Daddy…" Shanice said softly. "You got a few minutes? "Always. What's going on?" She hesitated, chewing the corner of her thumbnail before answering. "I've been thinking a lot lately. About my purpose. My dreams. In addition, I realized—I have never really faced the things standing in my way. I've always tried to avoid the hard stuff, hoping it'd just… disappear."

"Mmm," Carlos hummed, knowingly. "That's a big realization, Shanice. Many folks never even get to that point. They run from the hard things and wonder why they stay stuck." "I get that now," she whispered. "But it's scary. Every time I try to take a real step toward what I want, I feel like something pushes back. Moreover, I just freeze. I don't know how to fight through it."

Carlos was quiet for a moment. Then he spoke with a calm strength that settled her spirit. "Real dreams—God-given dreams—always come with resistance," he said. "Obstacles don't show up to block you. They show up to *build* you. They're asking, *'How bad do you want this?'* and *'Are you willing to become the person who can carry this dream?'"*

Shanice felt something rise in her chest—a strange mix of fear and hope. "So you're saying I have to go *through* the obstacles...not around them? "Exactly," he said. "Anchoring yourself means standing your ground—even when everything around you is shaking. It means facing what scares you, what has hurt you, and what has tried to define you. That's where your strength is made." She could feel tears pressing at the corners of her eyes. "I've never done that before," she confessed. "I've always avoided conflict. I did not want to rock the boat... or disappoint people. But now I think I've been disappointing myself."

Carlos sighed, gently and reassuringly. "That's a powerful truth to admit, sweetheart. In addition, listen—it is never too late to stop running. Every obstacle you face is just one more tool God uses to shape you. Do not be afraid of it. Walk through it."

Her voice trembled. "You really think I can do it?"

"I *know* you can," he said firmly. "And more importantly, I know *God's* walking with you. You are not doing this alone. Anchor yourself in the truth, and take the next brave step."

Shanice closed her eyes and let those words wash over her. Her shoulders relaxed. Her heart slowed. Something inside her shifted.

"Okay," she said finally. "No more running. No more hiding. I want to be anchored… and free."

A smile warmed Carlos's voice. "That's my girl. You're already on your way."

That night, after they hung up, Shanice sat in silence for a long time. She did not have all the answers. She was not sure what obstacles she would face next. However, for the first time in a long time, she was not afraid of them. She had moment anchored her. And that was enough.

FOUR

God is Always Up to Something

"And Joseph's master took him, and put him into the prison, a place where the king's prisoners were bound: and he was there in the prison. However, the Lord was with Joseph, and shewed him mercy, and gave him favor in the sight if the keeper of the prison. And the keeper of the prison committed to Joseph." Genesis 39:7, 20-22.

Clearly, God was using Potiphar's wife for a purpose. Interesting enough, Joseph was already in Potiphar's house, but Potiphar's wife did not notice him. However, it was, after these things, that she cast her eyes upon Joseph. The temptation came after God established Joseph as a goodly person and well favored. Joseph resisted the temptation, and did not yield to fear, pride, or lust of the flesh.

Now, Joseph had to suffer the trial of lies and false accusations. Potiphar's wife was a woman in a rage. She turned against Joseph and rejected him. She set out to humiliate him and hurt him as much as she could. She attempted to create prejudice against him as Hebrew. She also attempted to destroy his reputation and character, by stating that he had raped her. Joseph now suffered the loss of everything that he had gained - his possessions and position. Potiphar's wrath fell unto Joseph. Potiphar imprisoned Joseph in fetters and irons. Potiphar placed

Joseph into political prison. Potiphar placed Joseph in the prison where the jailor gave him charge as the overseer **[Genesis 40:3]**. Potiphar did not plan to release Joseph.

Joseph had to have questioned God about the injustice of his imprisonment. He had obeyed God and done the right thing. He had not yielded to pride, fear, or lust of the flesh. He had demonstrated to Potiphar that he was a man of integrity. Why would Potiphar not believe him? Why did God not do something to keep him out of prison? Joseph had already experienced the grief and agony of a slave. Now, his situation was far worse. Joseph was now a prisoner. Even though Joseph demonstrated consistent faith, hard work, obedience, and flawless integrity.

Joseph learned a valuable lesson about endurance and hardship. In future years, he would be chief administrator over all of Egypt. He was to have complete control over the food supply. To be a just and compassionate administrator, he would have to know what it felt like to lose everything. This was a lesson that Joseph had to learn and learn well. Compassion, endurance, and hardness would all be necessary to lead Egypt through its economic collapse. Egypt would face with a seven-year famine.

We will all experience this type of suffering at one time or another. Sometimes, it seems like God is leading us into a trap. We go from a successful situation to calamity. It happens so fast that we wonder how did this happen. It is the doctor's prognosis of a serious disease when we are in peak condition. It is the closing of a company, after we have established ourselves with a successful career track. It is the loss of a loved one or divorce. These situations of suffering will occur on your way to achieving your dreams.

One of the greatest revelations that Shanice had while persevering toward her dream is that God is always up to something. God has an agenda for our lives. God will make sure that we are properly prepared to handle every situation.

God will make sure that we are properly prepared to handle every situation in our future

He proves us each step of the way. God allows the devil to test us to see whether we can be faithful over the small things before He elevates us to greater things. Every level that we climb becomes more challenging. These tests grow from small trials to sufferings. I have learned that God is not tempting us, but allowing the devil to test us. Just like a high school teacher gives test to their students.

God allows the devil to test us. The high school teacher use the tests to calibrate whether we have learned all of the total elements of the subject. God works in a similar way. However, these tests are not for His benefit. These tests are to help us determine our spiritual maturity. When we awaken to the reality that we fall short, we attempt to get closer to God. We seek Him out, and gain even greater trust in Him.

God was up to something with Joseph. God was preparing Joseph by teaching him to have a positive attitude while dealing with severe circumstances. As Christians, we must understand that some suffering is required on our journey to achieving our dream. God uses suffering to make us, settle us, and to strengthen us **[I Peter 5:10]**.

This Scripture is such a wonderful revelation. Suffering is for our good. Suffering matures, settles, and strengthen us. God strengthened Joseph and helped him. Joseph learned to maintain a positive attitude, which led to a deeper trust and commitment to God. Joseph learned the qualities of leadership in hard and difficult times,

You cannot be fair weather Christians. You should try to remain steadfast and unmovable through your difficult times. Your difficult times might last for a few weeks or few years. However, you have to learn that the longer the suffering, the greater the reward.

The warden of the prison began to notice Joseph. The warden saw that Joseph was a capable and a hard worker. The warden also noticed that Joseph's God blessed everything Joseph did. Therefore, the warden made Joseph overseer over all of the other prisoners.

Please notice that Joseph was in the lowest position that a man can find himself in jail. Joseph shows us the benefit of trusting in God and holding on to your dream, even in severe circumstances. His strong determination demonstrates that God will bless us no matter where we are and regardless of our trials and circumstances. God blessed Joseph and made everything he did a success.

Therefore, you must believe God and His Word. God will use the trials of your life and your blessings to make you better. More importantly, God wants you to become a good steward of your dreams. Therefore, you should count it all joy when your suffering comes. It will make you a better person, a better family member, better citizen, better co-worker, and a better Christian. Upon achieving your dream, you will be a wonderful steward of what God has provided for you. Your suffering may seem difficult. However, you should not lose focus. While going through your suffering, you must stop and not become discouraged. You must get up and go to work. You must work even harder and more diligently than those around you must **[Colossians 3:23-24]**.

In your suffering, you have to be a person of high character with a great positive attitude. You must know and believe that God is using your suffering to prepare you for something greater – your dream.

God was also up to something else. God had to make sure that Joseph remained successful in all kind of situations. God was also preparing Joseph for a position of second in rule in Egypt. Then and only then would the Egyptians allow Joseph and his family to settle in Goshen. God could thereby fulfill his promise to Abraham, Isaac, and Jacob. God promised Abraham that He would be a great nation. Joseph's progression toward his dream was also an instrument that God was using to fulfill a promise.

Each of our lives touches someone else. Everything that we can do and will affect someone else's destiny. Our willingness to pursue our dreams hinders God from achieving all of His purposes. When we are tempted to stop or not even start making, we are hindering God from working a greater plan **[2 Corinthians 4:17-18]**.

We must understand that the fulfillment of our dream is only the means to an end. God is a God of promise. If we were in Christ, we are Abraham's seed. Therefore, the fulfillment of our dreams allows God to keep His promise

49

to Abraham. God sealed this promise to Abraham in a blood covenant. This means that God cannot change His mind, and not fulfil His promise. Both heaven and earth can pass away, but God's word cannot change. This is the confidence that we should have about our dreams. Since God promised Abraham He would bless his seed. We have a guarantee that God will allow us to achieve our dreams.

When you are moving toward the fulfillment of your dreams, you must remind yourself that God is up to something. God is attempting to perform a greater work through you. God wants to use those things that He invested in you for the fulfillment of His promise. God selected you as a vessel to exalt you for His glory. What a wonderful blessing! You should come to the revelation that God is using you to accomplish His divine will. The achievement of your dreams allows His will to happen. To God be the glory!

Faithful Steps Forward: Trusting God's Hand in the Journey toward Your Dreams

When you are moving toward the fulfillment of your dreams, it is easy to get absorbed in the pace, the pressure, and the uncertainty of what lies ahead. However, in those moments, it is crucial to remind yourself that *God is up to something*. Your dream is not just about personal fulfillment—it is a part of a divine strategy. God is performing a greater work *through* you, not just for you.

God never plants a dream without a purpose. He does not stir up desire, passion, and vision in your heart without the intention of fulfilling His promise. Every step forward, no matter how small, is a faithful step toward something bigger than you imagined. Often, we look at progress through a human lens—metrics, milestones, and measurable results. However, God looks at obedience, faith, and trust.

Faithful steps forward require a commitment to believe that what God has deposited in you is not random. The gifts, talents, passions, and even your unique life experiences are all part of a holy blueprint. God invested in your future because He has already written it. He is calling you to walk boldly into what He has already prepared.

Sometimes, the journey feels slow or uncertain. Doubt creeps in. You wonder if the dream was too big or if you misunderstood what God was saying. However, the truth is that the delays, detours, and difficulties are not signs of defeat—they are often proof of development. God uses every season to shape your character, deepen your trust, and clarify your purpose.

Taking faithful steps forward means saying *yes* to God, even when you do not see the whole picture. It means showing up consistently, praying when you do not have the answers, and serving when you feel unseen. It is writing the vision down, even when you do not have the resources. It is preparing the presentation, the plan, or the proposal, even when no one has yet given you a platform.

Joseph had a dream, but before the dream became reality, he experienced betrayal, slavery, and prison. Still, he kept moving. David, as anointed king had to wait years before wearing a crown. He often hid in caves. Yet he kept moving. Jesus, the ultimate example, walked faithfully toward the cross, knowing it would lead to resurrection.

Faithful steps forward are not always flashy. Sometimes, they are quiet decisions, tearful prayers, or difficult choices. However, they are always powerful. Each step says, "God, I trust You more than I trust what I see."

So today, as you move toward the dream in your heart, remind yourself: *God is up to something.* He is working behind the scenes. He is using every moment, every gift, and every trial to fulfill His promise. And as you take faithful steps forward, know this: your obedience is unlocking the very thing you have been praying for. Keep walking. God is with you, and His plan is unfolding.

FIVE

Learn How to Wait for Your Success

The sun had just begun its slow descent behind the city skyline as Shanice stepped into the cozy bistro on the corner of Eighth and Main. The warm smell of garlic and roasted herbs wrapped around her like a hug. She spotted Claudette seated in the far corner, sipping something warm from a ceramic mug.

Claudette was the kind of friend who did not just listen—she *heard* you. She had a way of pausing, tilting her head just so, and letting silence make space for whatever you needed to say. Tonight, Shanice needed that space. "Girl, you're glowing," Claudette said teasingly as Shanice sat down.

"I think that's just the candlelight," Shanice chuckled, but she knew it was more than that. Something inside her had shifted. Not completely, not perfectly—but enough. Once they ordered, Claudette leaned in. "So what's up? You said you had something on your heart."

Shanice took a breath and smiled softly. "I talked to my dad the other night. I needed to. I was struggling with how stuck I have been feeling, as no matter how hard I try to chase my dreams, something always pushes back. Moreover, for the first time, I admitted to him... I have been avoiding obstacles. Like really avoiding them."

Claudette's brow lifted with gentle curiosity. "And what did Carlos say?" "That I've been looking at obstacles the wrong way. That they are not just blocks—they are builders. Tools. Tests. He said they ask you if you're ready to carry the weight of your dream." Claudette nodded slowly. "That sounds like Carlos. Wise and gentle."

Shanice smiled. "Yeah... he helped me see that I've spent so much time running from what's hard because I didn't want to fail or disappoint people. But in doing that, I've kind of disappointed myself." There was a quiet pause between them, the weight of truth resting gently on the table. "I've started to realize something else, too," Shanice added. "It's not just about confronting obstacles. It's about learning to *wait*."

"Wait?" Claudette echoed, tilting her head. "Yeah," Shanice said, stirring her drink. "I've been so focused on trying to *make* things happen—rushing the process, pushing myself to prove something. However, I think success is not something you force. It is something you *grow into*. And that takes time." Claudette smiled warmly. "You're learning the art of holy patience."

"That's exactly what it feels like," Shanice said, her voice hushed. "I'm learning how to trust God's timing... how to prepare myself while I wait, instead of wasting the wait with frustration and comparison." "Shanice, that's powerful," Claudette said, reaching for her hand across the table. "Because waiting isn't passive. It is an act of faith. It believes that the seed *will* grow, even when you can't see anything yet."

Tears welled gently in Shanice's eyes, but they were the good kind that signaled healing, not hurt. "I'm learning that now. I do not want to rush past the process. I want to be ready when the door opens. I want to be *anchored.*"

"You will be," Claudette said with quiet confidence. "And when it comes, it won't just be success—it'll be fruit that lasts." They clinked glasses, not in celebration of a finish line reached, but in honor of a new beginning—a heart more willing to wait, work, and walk forward with courage.

Sometimes the most significant breakthrough does not come from movement—it comes from stillness. Shanice was learning that waiting was not a weakness. It was preparation. Moreover, her roots were growing deeper than ever before in that waiting.

Shanice began explaining to Claudette how the story of Joseph in the book of Genesis had brought her so much clarity. Claudette sat patiently, sipping on her sweetened iced tea and listening intently.

Joseph was prosperous while in prison. The Lord showed him mercy and favored him with the prison warden. The warden placed Joseph as the overseer of all activities in the prison. Joseph was also responsible for all of the prisoners. Whatever the jailor of the prison gave authority to Joseph. Neither did the warden check up on Joseph. Joseph had full autonomy to make decisions. Only the loving hands of God could make this happen. However, God had to teach Joseph a lesson on waiting. God used Joseph's prison experience to teach him to forgive and wait patiently for His timing.

It is not easy to wait. By nature, we want instant gratification, a quick response, and a speedy recovery. Mentors teach us how to make things happen quickly and proactively. Our ability to get results fosters our careers. Usually, the expectation is to obtain these results in short order. We are taught to be competitive. We must hurry up to beat our competition for the next promotion or job assignment. However, our rush to get these things done does not impress God.

God's nature is to do everything decently and in order. He takes no shortcuts. Even when we are going through our suffering, it seems as if God is taking His time. We occasionally ask, why does it take God so long? If God could create the world in six days, why does it take months or even years for God to move in our lives? What is holding up the fulfillment of our dream?

Despite his success, Joseph remained in prison. He was no doubt suffering in chains for a long time. Potiphar was in charge of the prison. Joseph supposedly attacked Potiphar's wife. The warden noticed Joseph's hard work over the period before he would have made him overseer of the other prisoners. Now, please think of the suffering, pain, and agony of having his feet and ankles shackled with fetters and chains. Even though the jailor took him out of the chains, he was still in prison. Why was Joseph in prison? Shouldn't his accomplishments and effort have given him a prison release? Why would God allow such a thing to continue? We have all asked these questions as we continue our struggles.

The importance of learning how to wait cannot be overemphasized. Waiting allows God to accomplish an even greater work in us. God has a plan. He plans to spend whatever time necessary to "prune" us. The time required for God to "prune" us depends on us. When we are willing to seek God's guidance, He keeps our steps. Occasionally, we become doubters, hasty, and seek ways to solve our problems. Then, we become stalled and make no progress. Learning to wait makes us perfect. God makes us wait to accomplish molding our nature into His likeness. We cannot truly fulfill our dream until we take on the nature of God.

Waiting allows God to do even a greater work in us. He wants to fulfil what He started in you.

The Pharaoh imprisoned his chief butler and chief baker in the Pharaoh's prison. Both men were chief officials in their areas and worked within the palace. The jailor assigned Joseph the duty of serving and caring for their needs. He served them for a long time. The bible indicates that Joseph served for a season while he was waiting. Why does God make us wait? Waiting teaches us humility, courage, and forgiveness.

Humility

God used Joseph's prison experience to teach the importance of humility and asking for help. Joseph became stronger through humility. In **Genesis 39:14**, Joseph asked the cupbearer to remember him, to show kindness, and for the cupbearer to ask Pharaoh for his release. Joseph had pride, arrogance, deceit, and haughtiness earlier in life. Joseph's father favored Joseph over his brothers because of his unusual management ability. Despite his young age, Jacob had made Joseph overseer of his other brothers.

Therefore, God had to humble Joseph's heart and season his character. This was happening as God made Joseph wait for his release from prison. God created a contrite spirit within Joseph.

Humility is an absolute necessity in life. The humble person does not attribute to himself any goodness or virtue that he does not possess. He does not overrate himself or take immoderate delight in himself. A person of humility realizes his imperfections and acknowledges that all of his goodness, accomplishments, and good works come from God's grace **[Proverbs 16:19]**.

You will never achieve your dream without a true spirit of humility. When God has you waiting, He is teaching you to learn humility. As a Christian, you have just as many shortcomings as others. You should never walk around with a spirit of pride or arrogance. No matter our gift or level of anointing, not one of us is better. When you learn to wait, you let your suffering prisons humble you. You should not be concerned about defeat or humiliation. While enduring, God continually watches over you **[Romans 12:3]**.

Even Christians exaggerate about their blessings. They want others to think that they have the favor of God. They purchase new cars, houses, and other tangible assets to demonstrate their relationship with God. Many times, they are incapable of paying for these things. They become indebted and suffer needlessly. Proverbs says that the blessings of the Lord make one rich and have no sorrow.

This is the actual test of whether God has given us favor. When we do not have a humble spirit, God sees this behavior as pride. Therefore, you must accept your status because your status is only temporary. God is capable of elevating you in due season. However, God wants you to acquire humility.

Jesus demonstrated the highest level of humility. He was willing to leave His home in glory and suffer the shame of the cross for us. Jesus allowed the Lord to use him completely. Even though He was God, He was tempted and suffered as we do. Now, He is sitting at God's right hand. This is the type of humility that God requires of us. God uses our suffering to create this type of humility. God will continue to incubate us until we become humble. I have witnessed many people experience extreme suffering. They lost completely everything, including their health. They cried out and prayed to God, but maintained their pride. Eventually, God broke their high-minded spirit. After being humbled, God used them as a living testimony and example of a model Christian.

Humility proves to God our intentions. God rewards the humble in spirit. With humility comes riches, honor, and life. "By humility and fear of the Lord are riches, honor, and life." [Proverbs 22:4].

Humility brings true religion, which is expressed by fear of the Lord. Pride hinders true religion. The fear of the Lord is the feeling of dependence, a lowly opinion of self, and the surrender of the will. The fear of the Lord is the source of every blessing. Humility is difficult to acquire. It is so essentially different from weakness. Humility allows us to press forward energetically without thought of self or admiration from the world. God rewards us with riches, honor, and life. When justice is done, the best man will receive the best reward. The humble who do not seek honor shall have it. The first shall be last, and the last shall be first.

Shanice sat on the edge of her bed, her Bible still open and tears brimming in her eyes. She had just finished reading **Philippians 2:5-11**, and the words had pierced her heart in a way they never had before. For the first time, she saw humility not as a sign of weakness or mere modesty, but as the very posture of Christ, the King who willingly knelt, served, and surrendered out of love. Overwhelmed by this revelation, she picked up her phone and called her sister.

"Hey, Jen," Shanice said, her voice trembling slightly.

"Hey, sis! You okay?" Jennifer responded, sensing something different in her tone.

"I'm good… I just had a moment and need to share it with you." Shanice paused, gathering her thoughts. "I've always thought humility meant thinking less of yourself, keeping quiet, not taking up space. However, today, I saw it differently. Jesus chose humility. He had all power and all glory, but He emptied Himself—not because He was weak, but because He was strong enough to love that deeply. That kind of humility is powerful."

Jennifer was silent for a moment, letting Shanice's words sink in. "Wow," she finally whispered.

"And it hit me," Shanice continued, "God doesn't just commend humility—He *dwells* in it. When we humble ourselves, we make space for Him. It's not about denying who we are but embracing who He is through us."

Another quiet moment passed between them, filled with awe and reverence. "You always have something deep to share when I need it most," Jennifer said softly. "Thank you."

Shanice smiled through her tears. "Just walking with Him," she replied. "He keeps showing me more."

Courage

Joseph became stronger through courage. God used his prison experience to teach him about truth. When the chief baker inquired about the interpretation of his dream, Joseph gave him a truthful interpretation. Joseph told the chief baker that he would die within three days. This act by Joseph took a lot of courage. Most likely, the chief baker had become Joseph's friend. However, Joseph had gained courage by learning how to wait. We often face situations that require us to share bad news. At such a time, we must remain courageous and truthful. We must not deceive people and have them have hope in God. Learning to wait is essential to gaining courage. God sees our waiting to show us that our difficult circumstances will not overcome us. Overcoming our difficult circumstances will not overcome us. Overcoming our difficult situations builds courage **[Psalms 118:6]**. We discover through waiting that God was with us all the time.

Jennifer took a deep breath, letting Shanice's revelation settle in her heart before responding. "You know, that touched me," she said gently. "And it connects to something I've been thinking about too—courage." Shanice listened closely as Jennifer continued. "Lately, I've realized that courage isn't the absence of fear, it's the decision to keep going even when fear is present. And I've been learning that true courage comes from knowing that God is with us, not just when we're strong, but especially when we're not." Her voice was steady and reassuring. "Shanice, God has always been with you—through the quiet seasons, the hard ones, and even in moments like today, when your heart is open and your spirit is tender. He is there. You're never alone."

Shanice's breath caught in her throat, overcome by the comfort in Jennifer's words. "Thank you," she whispered. "That means more than you know." Jennifer smiled on the phone. "Sometimes we forget that God doesn't require us to have it all together. He wants us to trust Him enough to take the next step. That is courage. That's faith." Their conversation lingered for a while longer, filled with quiet affirmations and sacred reminders—sisters sharing not just blood, but a bond built on truth, faith, and the ever-present grace of God.

Patience

Joseph became stronger through his disappointments. Joseph's prison experience taught him to forgive and wait patiently for God's time. Joseph's interpretation of the chief baker and chief cupbearer happened. The chief baker was hanged, and the chief cupbearer was restored to his former position. However, the chief cupbearer forgot. The scripture does not explain why the chief cupbearer forgot about Joseph. Joseph had to remain in prison for two more long years. These two years must have been the most difficult years of all. Joseph must have had a high expectation about being released from prison. Every time the prison doors were opened, he had to expect that his deliverance had come. However, Joseph was forgotten in prison. He had to accept that the cupbearer would not help him. He would not get a chance to appeal his case before Pharaoh.

Joseph could have easily become depressed and despondent. The chief cupbearer was someone in high places who had no power to help him, but he forgot about Joseph immediately after being released from prison. This type of treatment had occurred before in his life.

The people closest to him had failed him: his brothers, Potiphar, and now the chief cupbearer. They all failed and disappointed him. However, God would use these disappointments to teach him the art of learning to have patience. Notice that the Bible does not indicate that Joseph made any complaints. He never spoke to Potiphar about his wife's behavior or the charge of rape. Joseph remained silent. He was learning to forgive and wait patiently on God. God supplied Joseph strength in his time of trouble **[Psalms 27:14]**.

God will strengthen your heart to handle any problematic situation. You should expect God to deliver you. However, God expects you to wait until the appointed time.

Think about how often those closest to you have hurt and caused you pain. How frequently they may forget you and fail you. These people also mistreat you and cause suffering to occur in your life. Many times, the worst offenders are those in the body of Christ. Some Christians have made promises that they did not or cannot keep. They consistently fall short of your expectations. These disappointments often come from the people you have helped or loved most. They apologize to you, and continue to let you down. Paul's letters to the New Testament church apply to many churches today. You must learn to forgive when people forget you and mistreat you. You must learn to wait on God and not wait on people. These people include your loved ones, friends, and close acquaintances. People can help sometimes, but not always. Even if they help, they cannot always meet your needs. The only perfect help available for all circumstances is the help of God. You must learn to wait patiently upon Him.

You cannot rush your dreams. Learning to wait teaches you to have peace and contentment. Waiting is holding on to your dreams. You must be determined to allow God's plan to work out. God will not speed up your dreams because of your anxiety. God will not indicate the timing of your dream fulfillment. He guarantees that it will happen. Paul in Galatians advises us to be not weary in well doing, for we shall reap, if we do not give up. Not giving up is a key ingredient to holding on to your dreams. Dreams do come true. However, there is usually a time element. God has many things that He must orchestrate to ensure you are at the right place and time. Learning to wait ensures you do not move prematurely to accomplish your dreams. Waiting demonstrates your confidence in God. God will always keep His promise in His own time.

After thoughtful silence, Shanice spoke up again, her voice tinged with excitement. "You know who would love this conversation? Claudette." Jennifer immediately agreed. "Yes! We have not caught up with her in a while, and I know she would have something beautiful to add. She's been going through her journey with patience, hasn't she?" Shanice nodded, even though Jennifer could not see her. "Exactly. In addition, with what God has shown us about humility and courage, we need to sit down, share, and encourage each other. It's time." Jennifer added, "And we need to remind her—and ourselves—that dreams do come true. Sometimes it just takes humility to yield, courage to step forward, and patience to wait on God's perfect timing."

Without hesitation, they pulled up Claudette's number and called her. When she answered, laughter and warm greetings filled the line. Jennifer jumped right in. "Claudette, girl—we have *so* much to talk about. God has revealed some deep things to us, and we immediately thought of you."

Claudette's curiosity was instantly piqued. "Okay, now I'm intrigued! What's going on?"

Shanice chimed in. "It's about humility, courage, and patience that stretches your soul. We have had these moments with God; we know it is time to bring it all together. And we want to tell you something we both felt in our hearts—you need to know that dreams come true. Yours included."

Claudette's voice lit up. "Wow… I have been in a place where I have been praying about those exact things. Let's talk!"

They quickly decided on dinner that Saturday night at their favorite restaurant, a cozy spot that had hosted many of their heartfelt conversations over the years. As they locked in the plans, all three women felt an unspoken anticipation—God was weaving their journeys together for a purpose, and Saturday night would be more than just dinner. It would be divine alignment.

SIX

Dreams Do Come True

On Saturday night, Shanice, Claudette, and Jennifer gathered as promised, settling into a cozy corner with warm drinks and open hearts. As the conversation flowed, Shanice began to share a decisive shift in her mindset—an unshakable belief that dreams do come true. With a glowing sense of purpose, she explained how this revelation came from her deep study and reflection on the life of Joseph in the Bible. She spoke of his journey from the pit to the palace, from betrayal to blessing, and how his unwavering faith, even in the darkest moments, ultimately led to fulfilling his God-given dreams.

Shanice's words carried weight as she encouraged Claudette and Jennifer never to let go of their dreams, no matter how distant or delayed they might seem. Together, they reflected on their lives and found renewed hope, realizing that if God could bring Joseph's dreams to pass, He could do the same for them. That night became more than just a meet-up—a moment of revelation, inspiration, and deep sisterhood rooted in faith and purpose.

The atmosphere felt charged with something more profound than casual conversation as the evening settled around them. Shanice leaned forward, her voice calm but full of conviction. "I've been studying Joseph's life," she said, her eyes steady. "And what I've learned has changed everything for me. His journey wasn't easy—he was betrayed, forgotten, even falsely accused—but he held onto the dreams God gave him." Claudette and Jennifer listened intently, their expressions shifting as Shanice continued. "I realized that just because a dream takes time doesn't mean it's denied. God's timing is perfect. Joseph waited years, but in the end, he saw every dream fulfilled."

Jennifer nodded slowly, the weight of her unspoken dreams surfacing. "It's easy to forget that God is still working in the waiting," she whispered. Claudette added, "Sometimes I wonder if I've missed my chance. But hearing this—it's like God is reminding me not to give up." Shanice smiled warmly. "That's exactly it. If God did it for Joseph, He can do it for us. We must believe, even when it doesn't make sense."

In that sacred moment, hope began to rise again. Their hearts reconnected with dreams they had buried or dismissed. The room was filled with a quiet reverence, as each woman felt the presence of something greater—faith being reignited. What started as a simple gathering became a divine appointment, a sisterhood circle marked by revelation, encouragement, and the shared belief that God is still in the business of making dreams come true. Shanice expounded further on her overwhelming new insight.

God strengthened Joseph to serve an additional two years in prison. He had learned some valuable lessons in Egypt. He had a better life perspective and a closer relationship with God. He discovered that detours do lead to destiny. God had ordered his steps. Joseph also learned that obstacles would not stop you because God is always up to something. His most valuable lesson was learning to wait.

He was captive in prison while the chief cupbearer was set free. Joseph had proven to God that he was now ready. He had been "pruned," and was now prepared for his success.

God works to purge and strengthen us. We cannot escape God's effort to "prune" us. He intends to make us more productive. God will not give us our dreams so that we can become unproductive. He expects us to be ready and willing to bear much fruit. This is how God gets glory out of our lives. Using our dreams to bear more fruit draws men unto Him [St. John 15:2]. Joseph was now ready to bring forth more fruit for the glory of God.

God disturbed Pharaoh through a dream. However, Pharaoh could not interpret the dream. In his dream, Pharaoh stood by the River Nile. Suddenly, seven well-fed cows came out of the river and began grazing among the reeds by the bank. Then, all of a sudden, seven thin, poorly fed cows came up out of the Nile and stood by the well-fed cows. The dream startled Pharaoh, and he woke up.

God disturbed Pharaoh a second time with the dreams. He felt sure there was some significance. Therefore, he called all the magicians and wise men to the palace. Not even one could tell Pharaoh what the dreams meant. God has the power to make men fail in meeting a need. There is every indication that God was blocking the minds of Egyptian magicians and wise men. God was working behind the scenes to work things out for His servant Joseph and the children of Israel. Jacob and his family could not foresee the economic crisis that would devastate the land. However, God is always looking ahead into the future.

God always works behind the scenes to move us closer to our destiny. He uses every event as a means to an end. God will even make the most intelligent and effective mean fall to give His servants glory. The wisdom and power of God are infinite in helping us **[Romans 11:33-36]**.

God stirred the chief cupbearer to remember Joseph. The cupbearer was most likely standing there watching everyone fail in interpreting the dream. Then, suddenly, he remembered Joseph. After two long years, the cupbearer told Pharaoh about Joseph. Joseph had interpreted the dream of the chief baker and him, and everything happened just as he said. The cupbearer suggested that Pharaoh call for Joseph. We must never forget that God causes a chain of events to occur. God had already worked out things for Joseph and His people. God can stir the minds and hearts of people to help us. We all have experienced situations where we received some unexpected help. Many times, the help was from strangers. We must remember that these events are not accidental. Sometimes, those with less experience, maturity, or anointing help us.

The hand of God orchestrates our every step. God uses people to help us achieve our dreams. God places people in particular places in our lives or puts us in them. Then, God uses these people to help us achieve our goals or help us through a circumstance.

Shanice realized that God placed many people to help her in her endeavors. Sometimes, it was a senior Executive, and other times it was a custodian, office secretary, or church member. Each would encourage her to talk to certain people or consider certain aspects of her work.

Usually, it was a casual conversation. It always seemed odd at first. Later, she realized that God was working behind the scenes.

God had Joseph released to stand before Pharaoh. Joseph was standing before the most powerful ruler in the world and his officers. Pharaoh came straight to the point. He told Joseph his dreams and that no one could interpret them. Joseph declared that he had no ability or power to help, but God did. Joseph said that God would help Pharaoh by giving him the meaning of his dreams. He acknowledged that only God could help in this situation. Joseph interpreted the dreams, and Pharaoh released him from prison.

God only delivers us from our trials and circumstances after properly preparing. We must be ready to endure our trials to make us better people and more diligent stewards of our dreams. Before our dreams can come true, God must test us. God's process is not an easy one. We are ready to meet any challenge when we graduate from God's process. "But He knoweth the way that I take; when He has tried me, I shall come forth as pure gold." [Job 23:10].

God gave Joseph the ability to advise Pharaoh and to show him how the need could be met. Joseph recommended that Pharaoh find a qualified administrator and put him in charge of the land of Egypt. God had created the situation for Joseph. Each step in Joseph's journey prepared him to assume this new position. Even Joseph's recommendation to find a capable administrator was orchestrated by God. When we are ready to take stewardship of our dreams, God will put the right words in our mouths. Remember, it is the spoken word that creates action. [Luke 21:15].

71

The advice Joseph gave was sound wisdom, and Pharaoh recognized it. Joseph also spoke with authority in his recommendation. What happened next was a miracle! A natural man would see Joseph's transformation as a rags-to-riches story. Joseph was transformed from an enslaved person to a servant, a prisoner, and now a ruler. The dreams that Joseph had told his family had become a reality. Despite his suffering, he held on to his dreams. God kept His promise. Then, Pharaoh acknowledged the God of Israel. Pharaoh realized that God had revealed all this to Joseph.

When it happened, Joseph was exalted over all the people of Egypt. Joseph was put in charge of the king's palace. Everyone except Pharaoh was subject to him. He was second in command over all of Egypt and the entire land. Pharaoh exalted him with the symbols of full authority. Joseph was given the ring of the Pharaoh, royal linen, a gold chain, and the second chariot behind Pharaoh. Pharaoh decreed that he was the first ruler, but Joseph was the second.

God has the power to bless you in marvelous ways. However, you must make yourself available to God. You must believe Him, obey him, and follow him with all your heart. God will pour His power into our lives. You must continue to see yourself as chosen. You are not a dreamer, but you do have a dream. Hold on to your dreams, and God will exalt you in due season. **[St. John 15:16].**

God wants you to bear fruit. The achievement of your dream is the bearing of the fruit. When God blesses you with fruit, it remains. Your fruit will not wither away, because God gave it. Fruit is one of God's ways of allowing men to see our good works that glorify Him. God receives the glory when you achieve your dream, especially when you have pleaded your cause to Him. So, hold on and do not let go!

As their chat ended, Shanice leaned back in her chair with a soft smile, her eyes shining with clarity. "You know," she said, "I've been chasing this dream for so long and tonight it finally clicked—God *wants* me to bear fruit. The dream I have been praying about is not just for me. It's the fruit He's planting through me to glorify Him."

Claudette nodded, emotion catching in her throat. "That part right there hit me, too. When the blessing comes from God, it *remains*. It does not fade or fall apart. It lasts. Moreover, I have seen that — the things I tried to do on my own never lasted, but the things I surrendered to Him. They're still bearing fruit."

Jennifer added, "And it's not just about what we accomplish—it's about *who sees God through it*. Our fruit is how the world sees His hand on our lives. When people look at what we have overcome, built, and held on to by faith, they see His glory. That's the point of it all."

Shanice leaned forward, her voice firm. "So we hold on even when it's hard. Even when it feels delayed. Because when God brings the dream to pass, it's not just our victory—His testimony." Claudette smiled. "Exactly. Our dreams are seeds, but the fruit. That is His evidence. In addition, He makes sure it lasts. "Jennifer nodded. "So we don't let go. Not now. Not ever."

SEVEN

Now That Explains It

As Shanice drove home, the warmth of the evening still wrapped around her like a soft blanket. The conversation, prayers, and hugs all left her feeling seen, strengthened, and understood. However, a more profound thought settled in her heart as the streetlights flickered past her windshield. Now that explains it," she whispered, her fingers gently gripping the steering wheel. Joseph did not just have favor with people—he had favor with God. That was the difference. That is why his dream did not die, even in the pit or the prison. God saw his heart.

She reflected on how easy it is to receive admiration by people, liked, praised, and even promoted. Now more than ever, she knew that divine favor—God's approval—was what truly mattered. Some people have big dreams but lack the character to carry them. They chase success without surrender. They want the spotlight without the sanctification. However, Joseph was different. In addition, that is what I want to be—different, favored in heaven, not just known on earth. Shanice smiled quietly, her soul at peace. "God, keep me in your eyes. That's where my dream lives." Shanice could see how Joseph conquered his challenges.

Joseph found favor not only in the eyes of God but also in the eyes of men. Unfortunately, the eyes of God eliminate so many from achieving their dreams. A person may have favor with men, but be a heathen in the eyes of God. We all know people who have dreams but lack moral character and love for God. They attempt to fulfill their dreams through manipulation and shortcuts. Their only concern is to benefit themselves and their immediate circle of acquaintances. This attitude falls way short of why God wants us to achieve our dreams. The Bible tells us that our success is not based on our power or might, but God's Spirit.

Joseph is listed in God's Hall of Fame in the eleventh chapter of Hebrews. Joseph committed himself to God and to following the promises of God. Once he committed to God, he never wavered or slipped back. He stuck to the end very well. Joseph was captive for many years. He spent almost half of his life away from his family. He had never been able to confront his brothers over the evil they had done him. Yet, Joseph had forgiven them. The famine presented Joseph with the opportunity to reunite with his family.

Joseph showed that he had forgiven them for their evil ways. After Jacob had died, the brothers began to fear that Joseph might take vengeance against them. Therefore, the brothers sent a message to Joseph confessing their sins, asking for forgiveness, and offering themselves as servants. He demonstrated genuine love and forgiveness.

Once you have achieved your dreams, you must demonstrate genuine love and forgiveness. God used every event to prune you and give you a spirit of forgiveness. You can never be truly successful unless you have the spirit of forgiveness. Hatred will make you miserable and hinder you from enjoying your dreams. The spirit of forgiveness says, "Once forgiven, always forgiven. The old sin or wrong is never repeated. **[Romans 12:21]**.

Your commitment to following God will make you do nothing less. You must remember that it is God's place to judge, not ours.

God devoted twelve complete chapters to cover how He prepared and allowed Joseph to accomplish his dreams. Joseph endured affliction for fifteen years to reach his dream. However, the next fifty-four years are covered in five verses. These verses also explain why Joseph had to learn true love and forgiveness. These five verses also give us a revelation of God's divine purpose. Why had God raised Joseph to become second in command in Egypt? God allowed Joseph's success for two primary reasons. These reasons may shock you. One would think that God rewarded Joseph for enduring the suffering and hardship while being held captive in Egypt. We could also theorize that God was demonstrating that good would always overcome evil. However, God allowed Joseph to reach his true potential in the will of God, so that he could save the land of Egypt from total economic collapse and starvation during the seven-year famine. He could also bring Israel down to Egypt to fulfill his promise to Abraham. Finally, we see them from the worldly influence and intermarriage with the Canaanites.

After you have become successful, it would be easy to forget about the salvation of others. It would be easy to forget that God has given us benefits for achieving good. So, why does God allow us to achieve our dreams? **Reaching our dreams is really about God and His salvation**. We are one chess piece in God's game of chess.

Reaching our dream is really about God and His plan of salvation

Just like in chess, God is working to get us to kingship and win the game. He allows us to have successes and benefits to continue to further His kingdom. We reap the benefits, but God gets the complete glory. God will keep His promise and afford us the best that heaven has to give. But His determination is that every man might be saved. We must not think of our dream achievement in a selfish way.

We have to think of it as a larger purpose. God is attempting to save many people alive. God wants to work through us, and our ability, along with His investment of experiences, to help deliver others. God will allow us to enjoy great benefits as a reward. God will grant us peace, riches, and honor for the remainder of our lives. However, God wants everyone saved.

Joseph achieved his dreams so that God could save the entire Egyptian world from financial collapse. Joseph's genuine love for people and forgiveness of his brothers permitted him to accomplish both of God's purposes. God had overruled evil and worked it out for good. God had worked through Joseph to save God's chosen people, Israel, the believers of the earth. Joseph declared that he must repay evil with good. Joseph's declaration should define our nature. We must overcome evil by using the good that comes from achieving our dreams.

How did Joseph live the rest of his life? Joseph remained faithful to God. God had completed His primary purpose for Joseph by the time Joseph was fifty-six years old. He worked to keep his brothers together. He lived a godly and righteous life before the world of his day. Joseph was faithful to the end. Joseph was not only loyal but also fruitful.

The result was a tremendous blessing from God. God was giving fruit to Joseph's grandchildren, who were to become the future believers of God upon the earth, even Joseph's grandchildren. God received the glory!

Joseph held onto his dream until death. When he was 110 years of age, he faced death. As he was dying, Joseph wanted his brethren to know that the promises of God are true. God would keep them through all of their afflictions and, eventually, take them to the Promised Land. Even in his death, Joseph demonstrated his faith by demanding an oath from his brothers. He made them swear to carry his bones back to the Promised Land when they returned. This was one of the greatest declarations of faith in the promise of God.

This is an example of the ultimate sign of holding on to a dream. No matter how long it last, Joseph wanted to declare his faith in the most significant way he could. Throughout his life, he had given a strong witness to God. In death, Joseph wanted the same testimony. He wanted to declare with his bones that God makes dreams come true.

As Shanice pulled the covers over her and turned off the lamp, her thoughts lingered on Joseph's journey. The betrayal, the pit, the prison seemed like a series of detours, but tonight she realized they were divine steps. God was not just preparing Joseph for personal success but positioning him to preserve a people. That shifted something in Shanice's heart. Maybe her dreams were not just about her either. Perhaps they were about the lives connected to hers—the ones God had already marked for hope, deliverance, and destiny through her obedience.

She lay there quietly, the weight of the revelation settling in. All this time, she had been asking God to make her dreams come true, but now she saw God asking her to trust Him with a dream much bigger than God was asking her. It was not just about writing the book, starting the business, or launching the ministry. It was about what those dreams could unlock for others—the encouragement, the employment, the healing, the transformation. God was writing a story through her life; her willingness to walk it out could mean life for someone else.

With a whisper of prayer, Shanice surrendered her timeline, fears, and even her ambition. "Lord, use my dreams to fulfill Your plan," she said. There was peace in that surrender. Not the kind that comes from having all the answers, but the kind that comes from finally understanding your place in something eternal. As her eyes closed, she was not just hoping to reach her dream—she was resting in the truth that God's dream for her life was already in motion and beautiful.

EIGHT

A Certain Place for
A Certain Reason

Your reading this book is not an accident. It is by divine providence. I believe that God places us in certain places for a reason. Perhaps, this is your appointment with destiny. Alternatively, God may want you to share this little book with someone struggling with their dreams. Either way, God is letting you know that He wants you to reach your full potential in His will. Sometimes, our full potential is only realized through the testing of our faith. Therefore, God places us in certain places that will help us overcome our fears. His reason is always to work a blessing through us. In all cases, God is working a larger plan. We are only the conduits through which He works.

Joseph was taken captive so that he could be delivered to the place that would provide salvation for his family. However, Joseph being taken to Egypt was only part of a larger plan. God had maneuvered him to Egypt for even a greater purpose. God's reason was revealed to Joseph's great-grandfather Abraham **[Genesis 15:13-14]**.

God's ultimate plan for Joseph's arrival in Egypt was to make Israel a great nation. God prophesied that the children of Israel would be in bondage for 400 years, but would come out with great substance. In other words, God would let them remain captive for 400 years. When Israel left Egypt, they were rich. God placed Joseph in Egypt, so that the children of Israel would grow in size and ultimately leave Egypt with wealth that would take to the promise land.

God has assigned a certain place to you. God cannot work out the next steps in your destiny until you arrive in that certain place. Have you ever wondered why you were inspired or motivated to leave your hometown, a job, or even a church? When people quizzed you, or even challenged you, you had no good reason. Even if you had a reason, it was not a concrete one. It is simply because God wants you in that certain place. The reason may not be clear. However, you must have real faith that God is working all things together for you. The scriptures are full of examples. Accepting your present status is key to achieving your dreams. We cannot complain or murmur. Murmuring and complaining hinders our progress. We must accept the certain place as part of our destiny.

God has placed Shanice in some unusual places in her life. At that time in her life, she questioned everything that God was doing. She often asked God why this or that was happening. Why was she in this challenge or crisis? One day, God responded with why not. God has no respecter of person. God is just using us to accomplish His divine will. In the process, we receive unexpected blessings. More importantly, accepting our certain place puts us in position to receive our inheritance.

When you find yourself in certain places of challenges, we should rejoice. It is a demonstration that you have favor with God. You should not think that it is the devil. The devil cannot accomplish anything more than what God

81

allows. You should not believe your particular place is because of some sin. **[Romans 8:1]**.

Your current surroundings, relationships, job, and economic status are for a certain reason. God is attempting to accomplish something through you. God wants you to accomplish your dreams. This is how He accomplishes His divine will.

Shanice sat quietly on the edge of her bed, the weight of the past few weeks finally lifting as peace washed over her. It was not just relief—it was revelation. After all the striving, the confusion, and the moments where she nearly gave up, she finally understood: complete faith in God was the key to unlocking the dreams He had placed in her heart. Without hesitation, she reached for her phone and called Claudette.

When Claudette answered, Shanice did not waste a moment. "Claudette," she said, her voice a mix of awe and certainty, "I finally get it. Every place I have been in— every high, every low, even the stuff I did not understand—was a part of God's plan. Nothing was random. I had to go through it all to grow into the person I need to be for what's next." Claudette listened intently, sensing the shift in her friend's spirit. "I kept thinking I needed to control everything, to fix it all on my own. However, it was when I surrendered—fully, completely— that I started to see clearly. Faith does not just believe when things make sense. It's trusting God when they don't."

Claudette smiled on the other end. "I've been praying you'd see that, Shanice. God does not waste a single part of our journey. Even the broken places have purpose." Shanice sighed, this time not in frustration, but in release. "Yeah," she said, "I see that now. In addition, I am ready. Ready to walk this path not with fear, but with faith. Because if God brought me to it, He's already made a way through it." They sat in that sacred moment, letting the truth settle—two women, two hearts, connected by divine timing and the unshakable belief that every step has purpose when God is leading the way.

Claudette leaned back in her chair, the phone pressed gently to her ear as Shanice's words echoed with new understanding. She waited for a pause, and then spoke with a gentle conviction. "You know, Shanice," she began, "when I was going through my own season of confusion, trying to make sense of what God was doing in my life, He led me to the story of Joseph. I did not just read it—I lived in it for weeks. And the more I read, the more I realized how much it speaks to us dreamers."

Shanice listened intently as Claudette continued. "Joseph had these powerful dreams as a young man, dreams that didn't make sense to anyone around him. In addition, honestly, they did not even make sense to him at first. However, God was behind those dreams. In addition, even when Joseph was thrown into a pit, sold into slavery, lied on, and locked away in prison, the dream never died. Every part of his journey—just like yours—had purpose. The pit did not cancel the dream. The prison did not stop the promise. It all led him to the palace."

Shanice was silent for a moment, deeply moved. "So you're saying," she whispered, "even when life looks like it's falling apart, it could actually be falling into place?"

Claudette smiled. "Exactly. Joseph shows us that God's plan is always in motion, even when we cannot see it. And if we stay faithful, if we trust Him completely, our dreams can come true—not because we forced them to happen, but because we allowed God to bring them to life His way."

Shanice exhaled slowly, the connection between their stories stirring something deeper in her. "I needed that, Claudette. I really did. Maybe my pit moments were never about punishment—they were preparation." Claudette nodded, her heart full. "That's it, sis. God is not just the Giver of dreams—He is the One who brings them to pass. We just have to keep trusting the process."

NINE

Dreams do Come True

The room was cloaked in the deep, golden hues of the setting sun, shadows stretching long across the floor. Soft, swelling music — strings at first, low and haunting — began to stir in the background, almost imperceptible. Shanice stood still, silhouetted against the burning sky, her hands trembling slightly at her sides.

Slowly, she turned to Claudette, her voice cracking under the weight of everything she had carried. "Claudette..." she whispered, as the music grew just a little louder, the first piano notes striking like heartbeats, "I finally see it. Every broken dream... every closed door... it was not the end. It was the beginning. I wasn't being forgotten — I was being *forged.*"

Claudette, sitting motionless, her face bathed in fading light, said nothing. Her eyes shimmered with unshed tears as she watched Shanice fight her way into the realization she had waited so long to see bloom. Shanice took a trembling breath, her voice gaining strength, rising with the music. "I thought the silence meant God had abandoned me... but the silence was where He was *building me.* I thought the delays were a curse... but they were saving me from dreams I was not ready to hold. I thought the losses were killing me..." She paused, a tear breaking free, "...but they were resurrecting a woman I never knew I could become." The music swelled, deeper now, richer — violins soaring in the background.

Claudette rose slowly from her chair, crossing the space between them like a queen anointing a warrior. She placed her hands on Shanice's shoulders, steady and sure. "You were never losing," Claudette said, her voice fierce and trembling. "You were learning to *soar*. Every crack, every scar, every moment you thought you were drowning — it was the making of your wings."

Shanice choked back a sob, the music rising higher, a crescendo building in her chest. "The waiting wasn't the enemy," she said, her voice breaking into something wild and free. "It was the womb. It was the fire. It was the place where I became strong enough to carry the weight of the dream... without losing myself."

Claudette pulled her into a tight embrace, whispering into her ear, "And now you're ready. Now the world will see the flame that hell couldn't put out."

As they pulled apart, the final rays of sunlight disappeared, and the sky burst open with a thousand stars — the music reaching a powerful climax, full of triumph, full of destiny.

Shanice stepped forward into the night, head high, eyes blazing with unshakable faith. The dream was not ahead of her anymore — it was inside her. And she was ready to set the world on fire.

TEN

The Roadmap of Revelation

Holding on to your dreams is not about clinging to wishful thinking or chasing ambitions in your own strength. It is about recognizing that God plants dreams in the soil of our hearts, and through seasons of watering, pruning, and waiting, He brings them to life in His perfect timing. However, how do we navigate the journey? How do we make sense of the detours, delays, and divine setups? The answer is this: we use the Bible as our roadmap.

Throughout this book, you have walked with Shanice—a woman full of questions, uncertainty, hope, and a dream she dared to believe in. However, let us be clear: Shanice's story is not *the* story—it is only *an* example. Her journey, like that of her friends Claudette and others, was never meant to be a blueprint, but rather a beacon. A guide. A testimony. Their experiences serve to remind us that we are not alone, that faith still works, and that God still speaks, leads, and fulfills.

The Bible reminds us in **Hebrews 12:1** that we are "surrounded by such a great cloud of witnesses." These witnesses are men and women of faith—real people with real struggles—who trusted God through every chapter of their lives. Shanice stands among them as a modern reflection, but she, too, points us back to the greater witnesses found in Scripture.

87

Abraham shows us that even when the promise takes time, God is never late. Joseph teaches us that the dream may go through a pit and a prison before it ever reaches a palace. Esther proves that our positioning is no accident—God places us exactly where we need to be for such a time as this. Ruth reminds us that loyalty and perseverance unlock divine favor. Moreover, David's life tells us that God even crowns flawed people.

Then, above all, there is Jesus—the ultimate dream fulfilled. His life, death, and resurrection were the fulfillment of prophecy and the embodiment of purpose. Through Him, we see that surrender leads to glory, that suffering is never wasted, and that victory comes through obedience.

When we read the Bible, we do not just read history—we read identity. We read legacy. We read destiny. We begin to interpret our own lives through the lens of God's truth rather than through the confusion of our circumstances. Scripture becomes our compass when the way is unclear, our anchor when we feel unsteady, and our voice when we have lost the words to pray.

Therefore, as you continue your own journey—holding on to the dream that God has placed in your heart—do not rely solely on what you have read in this book. Let Shanice's story be a spark, but let the Word of God be your source. Dive deep into it. Ask God to speak to you through its pages. Discover your place among the great cloud of witnesses.

Because the same God who walked with them walks with you. The same God who fulfilled their dreams is faithful to fulfill yours.

This is not just the end of the book—it is the beginning of your breakthrough.

So keep holding on. Keep trusting the Author. He has not finished writing your story yet.

This is not just the end of the book — it is the beginning of your breakthrough. Every chapter you have lived through — the heartbreaks, the unanswered prayers, the silent seasons — has been leading you here, to the edge of something greater than you ever imagined. What felt like endings were really turning points, moments where the Author of your life was quietly setting the stage for a new and more glorious unfolding.

So keep holding on. Even when the pages seem blank and the silence feels heavy, trust that the Author is still at work. Keep trusting His hand even when you cannot trace His pen. The plot may twist, the road may darken, but His promise remains unshaken. He is the Master storyteller, weaving beauty from brokenness, triumph from trials, and hope from heartbreak.

He has not finished writing your story yet. No, this is only the beginning — the prologue to a destiny filled with purpose, promise, and power. The next chapters will not just restore what you lost; they will reveal a glory that far outweighs the suffering you endured. So lift your head. Turn the page. Take a deep breath and step forward with courage. The best part of your story is still to come — and it will be worth every tear, every prayer, and every moment you chose to believe when it would have been easier to give up.

The best part of your story is still to come — and when it unfolds, you'll understand why you had to cry those hidden tears, why you had to whisper those desperate prayers in the dark, and why you had to keep believing even when everything in you wanted to quit. Every tear you shed watered the seeds of your future. Every prayer you lifted became a brick laid on the path toward your destiny. Every moment you chose faith over fear, hope over despair, perseverance over surrender — it all mattered.

You will see that none of it was wasted. None of it was in vain. The silent battles you fought, the lonely nights you endured. The One who holds your future in His hands saw all some unseen sacrifices you made. In addition, when the breakthrough comes — because it *will* come — you will not just rejoice because you arrived; you will rejoice because you endured. You will look back and realize that the process did not break you — it built you. It did not bury you — it planted you for a greater harvest.

So hold your ground. Keep standing. Keep believing. What is ahead of you is greater than what is behind you. What is rising within you is stronger than what tried to take you out. The best part of your story will redeem every broken piece and illuminate every dark valley. Moreover, when it comes, you will know deep in your soul: it was worth it all.